MW00679017

Copyright © 2016, 2017, 2018
by Denver Day and Braswell Communications
Library of Congress Control Number:
2016954685
ISBN paperback: 978-0-9981763-0-7
ISBN ebook: 978-0-9906741-8-4

First Edition
Day, Denver D., Author
One, Otto, Editor
Braswell Business Communications Services Inc.,
Publisher

Literature is art, all dharma is fire, and this
copy of *Hipster Bricks: A Philosophical Novel*
is yours to keep. So, who are you?

Hipster Bricks is a fiction cut from whole
cloth. None of these events happened and I
invented the characters notwithstanding the
vigor of transcendental spirit, career
politicians, cold blooded killas, y
narcotraficantes.

Rev. date: December 2017

To order additional copies of the book contact
Braswell Business Communications Services Inc.
1-518-400-2729
www.fusepowder.com
www.denverday.com

David:

Please Enjoy

Hipster Bricks

this little
piece of
madness!
5/13/19
          - Dawn Dy

Hipster   Bricks

A   Philosophical   Novel

Denver   Day

Other books by Denver Day:
Pizza Noir No. 1:   Catch As Catch Can
Pizza Noir No. 2:   Alpha Taxonomy
Pizza Noir No. 3:   Pie In The Sky
The Only Game in Town

For Jules, who is both man and mouse.

sixty-nine.

Great lengths. I go to great
lengths to keep the peace. I would
walk a mile, if I thought it would help
me avoid dickering with any known
malignant bullshitter. Whoever isn't
with me is against me, that's a rule of
thumb about proper cause for making
certain snap judgments. Longer waiting
times for passing judgment can be worth
it, however, if the wait contributes to
useful class action policy against
recidivist assholes.

What is the name of the unfriendly
game when for one to speak at all, is
to relinquish some strategic advantage?
I can see enough to know it's a hustle;
at first I was surprised to note the
edge of prejudice embedded in such
attitudes. This mysterious antagonism
is based on bad intelligence, surely,
but why would anyone, without cause, go
to the trouble to distribute

disinformation about individuals?
Speaking as an ex-member of the working
press, I say misinformation presents
all sorts of civil difficulties.

   Maybe there is some otherwise
widely recognized point of conditioning
which I have missed entirely. For
starters, I really am a writer. That's
no joke, it's not a cover. And I'm a
talker. Words are a strong suit for
me, talking is part of my duty. I have
noticed a penalty assessment for
deviation from small talk among certain
factions, e.g. robots.

   I've noticed that many literary
portrayals of childlike tyrants are
allegorical of A.I. gone bananas.
Apeshit robot is as fine an explanation
as any for much of the world I had
encountered up to a certain point in my
life, down here in this fucking toilet.
But lately I've been learning. These
antique robots are mean and dumb. I

don't give a shit about their legacy
model, and their bad attitudes reflect
poorly on their designers.

Sometimes I wonder what, exactly,
people think they want from me, and of
how they've decided abuse is the best
thing to exchange for my mysterious,
yet-unnamed charity. Describing them
as automatons or hungry ghosts as we
may, they've still no cause for leaning
into me so closely. I have nothing so
intimate for them. In fact, these
entities are the very currency of which
they incorrectly believe themselves to
be bankrupt. So they surely do not
have any entitlement or proper use for
my script, for the likes of which many
people sell their souls.

Soul is generally a plurality.
Whenever I have cause to relocate, I
weigh the pending action in a universal
context. This is a key for carrying
adult responsibility. The body of

humanity can be thought of as a collective, therefore to be truly, optimally healthy, one must negotiate honest integration or at least some ethical standard for reconciliation among the community at large. Otherwise a person isn't being honest with themselves, or maybe they've fallen into some trap of solipsism.

Regularly, I encounter people who abuse the benefit of doubt, or if you will, the "human shield" which derives from the necessary collectivity of life and humanity. For example, I observe that most if not all transgressions against me come by way of group-think in bad faith, whether it's blindly accidental such as through the marketing of alcoholism to human children, or through intentionally malign vectors such as the cottage industry of identity theft. Such is this society today. People are known also to apply the fallacy of infinite

resources or "ecological shield,"
although it fares poorly as an excuse
amid post-colonialism.

I must persevere in subtle
teaching, and calm, peaceable personal
conduct unless I want to relinquish my
faith in humanity, which of course so
many have given up on before me. For
life in hell, is it honest to attempt
resembling whatever so many of these
miserable, shitty people hate? Maybe
such subterfuge is less than honest,
but it would be for safety's sake.
Honesty is physically dangerous because
so many people hate the truth.
Regardless of what I wear or where I
walk, I'll keep my boots on but tread
lightly.

Typically no one says, "Hey I do
not like you because of X-Y-Z." Maybe
if they knew why, they'd say it.
Sometimes trouble is taken to send an
envoy for providing some negative civil

assessment of the like. As to those
who would be happy to assault me, by
their own accord in the street, or
stand up and tell my face to fuck off
for no good reason, such an approach is
honest action therefore it's apart,
categorically, from the matter under
scrutiny here.

Anyway, it is clear that people
down here are tired, grouchy, mean, and
misdirected. The behavior is no wonder
or daresay defensible, because the
world often does nothing but mistreat
and lie. But hell, it does to me too,
my fundamental origins are no different
than anyone else's, and we all share
the same rights of way, no? Then, here
I encounter you, but this may not be a
common right of way. I am your
narrator here, the name's Rick. Hi
there.

sixty-eight.

16

Interaction with people occurs in the due course of conducting one's daily business. The line is fine between tolerance and alternatives to tolerance. A question arises of who and who not I'm willing to suffer. For instance, hustlers. Many hustlers are mean and hateful, much the way other people might hate you based on some various other predisposition of theirs. A claim of neutrality is often a lie. There is good with the bad, though, since some people actually aren't operating in bad faith. Find them.

A specific example? Ahh yes, my new friend who I met here in Phoenix, at a bar-slash-coffee shop co-located in the back end of a bookstore. As she shuffled a deck of cards expertly, I noticed a piece of yarn tied around one of the fingers. She displayed her incidental dangerousness honestly, which I appreciated as a demonstration

of an outfacing veracity that most
people don't possess, although it's
required for survival and enjoyment of
the world.

Even in hostility, there is a
stripe of honesty that I prefer to
uncalculating or lukewarm human agency.
Think of humanity as a social
parameter, the human condition. If it
isn't that, we ought not care if or who
is hostile or jesting. Without cause
for investigating some ostensible
measure, we wouldn't care and we'd
never know. In broad terms, people's
going out of doors always serves some
key social need. There are other
reasons too, but most loners are made,
not born. Maybe that is changing. I
admit it's been a long way since I last
left my dwelling for the sole and
expressed purpose of retrieving the
carcass of a caribou on behalf of the
tribe.

Maybe part of the problem derives from some social compromise in response to the dangers of strangers. Just looking around willynilly for a crowd to hang out with, can turn dangerous easily. Traditional social rules are often rooted in stone-aged politics that were designed to defend people from themselves. Such are the origins of concepts like "the other one" and "us and them."

Social compromise involves common pretexts of human interaction. Plainview determinations regarding who participates in such pretense is an interesting taxonomy. There is strong, unwritten, unspoken pressure to compromise ethical standards, and it leads many to sell their souls; Whole populations sell their entire volume of family stones, blindly so. A hustler successful in such a marketplace fails to retain ethical high ground, so high society amounts to a dustbin of goons.

By rights, station-minding is appropriate within a community. Beyond that, people ought to apply labels only very cautiously if at all. I recommend against it. Labels on people are usually incorrect, antiquated, and problematic if not dangerous. They divide, antagonize, and prevent peaceable interaction. The situation is abused widely in politics.

The group is not the individual, labels are a device of crowds, and crowds are cowards where individualists grow to be hated without due cause. For petty label-related reasons, fascinating organic relationships fail to develop, and ciphers linger despite being out-of-place agents in bad faith. Labels allow others to define things that people must define for themselves.

When interacting with others, in order to make a point and set an example, persistently I work to clear the air of presumptions or unsanctioned labels about myself, to the best of my ability. Such honesty does have a certain collateral cost for me, socially, although I would stop short of complaining. The practice helps me discover who is inclined to make prejudgment based on what can only be hearsay, forensically. Known unknowns of this approach include entropy among the marketplace of ideas, people's information sources, and their knowledge.

sixty-seven.

I should report that I'm an asshole, caveat lector. But I'm charitable, I really do give a shit about the welfare of total strangers. I could go on, as you are probably beginning to realize. And so I shall.

Denver Day

   "I am a charitable asshole." I
told my new friend with the finger
string.

   "What do you do for a living with
a credential like that?"

   "Its applications depend on the
circumstances. Circumstances such as
yourself, for example; How is it that
you came to be so good at shuffling
those cards?" It is truly a suspicious
talent, so it was a fair question. She
answered with a smile.

   "Seriously, I kill people for a
living." I said.

   "Who doesn't?"

   "Oh not really. Not yet."

   "And I'm not a whore."

   "Who isn't. What's your name?"

"I'm called Jules. What'll it be today? Longnecks are fifty cents until five."

"I will have five of those. Mexican or European lagers please."

"All at once? That's a lot of carbohydrates."

"Not really beer. But I would like some iced green tea."

"You hungry?"

"Maybe."

"I'll get your tea. Who are you?"

"Rick."

She didn't have to be there, but she was. That was my introduction to Jules, who had no real business doing

that job. Who cares why though, since
her robust joie de vivre was admirable;
And what's in a job? When dependent
origination sufficiently explains a
jewel like Jules among the dharma, the
philosophical question is solved. Nor
did I have any warrant for my station,
which at the time was that of a mid-day
bar patron.

The human condition compels me to
wander the universe looking for
incumbent comrades, hairless or not.
Jules was both. Hairless lizards don't
seem to giggle or fart as much as furry
mammals, which is why lizards make good
jailers or bankers. They're fully
content to lay low for three hundred
years while a kingdom crumbles in order
to vest themselves in the erstwhile
currency. Nobody squats quite like a
lizard. They have good jokes, however,
which they cook up during their long
periods of free time, so they make good
bartenders. Jules came back with my

tea.

"Care to join me in a cup?" I asked. She cared.

Nearly at the other end, six stools to my right there was one other body at the bar, enjoying some or another short order delight from the kitchen.

Jules returned with tea and sat down across the bar from me.

"So. Who might you kill? Are you going to kill me?"

"No. I don't want to. When I first meet a person, it's usually obvious to me whether they might be number one." I said.

"Most people are already dead anyway, as far as I can tell." she said.

"Death in the quick is always conditional, but dead people can still be killed." I said. "Death is a false idol but knows no limit in the house it abides."

"How is your tea?"

"Delicious, thank you. Quid pro quo, why are you here?" I asked.

"I get bored, and this fixes that. It's not for the money. People who worship death are the same ones who worship money. You?"

"My human condition compels me to wander the universe looking for incumbent comrades, hairless or not. This is good tea and getting better."

"Soup's on too. My recipe. You'll see, it's good shit."

I considered how this person, due to her boredom, had prepared soup for random strangers like me. Two minutes later I was diving into a tomato bisque with help from a stack of flatbread crackers.

sixty-six.

The world affects people differently. In me it has invoked an individualism whereby no higher authority apart from one's own political will is acceptable. However, there is a common misconviction that traditional authority is all that prevents certain, immediate universal doom. Together in any proportion, these two opposing perspectives are in conflict.

Authoritarian assemblage requires governance, incidental to which administrators often catastrophically fail, to realize and accommodate for the logical contradiction inherent in staffing a position at the top of a system whose rules dictate that one isn't in charge of oneself. The best case scenario for any meaningful policy that reckons with the organizational anachronism is silly, and begins the day with profanity and arbitrary class structure.

Meanwhile, people who've gone to the trouble to cultivate their own individualism don't suffer well the enforcement of bad logic. In a society where the mob is given any degree of sanctioned enfranchisement, people vested in rightful liberty will require institutional political quarter for protection from mob rule. There are various ways to respond to assaults by a class, as a class. Beware of those who enforce the tyranny of the majority, which is a known requisite for intellectual disenfranchisement.

Individualism is not a free ride,
freedom must be earned and updated
regularly. When people, whether mulish
or sheep-like, are led systematically
to slaughter in vicious cycles, it's a
natural dead-hand state of traditional
society; it's a manifestation of what
some ancient philosophies describe as
"hungry ghosts."

     If people can be helped out of
such a cycle, then they should be. If
not, they simply come of age believing
everything they're told. That may
sound like no big deal, perhaps coming
only at the minimum cost of losing some
would-be society of intellectuals. But
in the end, it probably won't get the
victim anywhere but finished, and
that's subjectively devastating; it's
a whole universe destroyed in the most
broad application of a clinical
abortion. One's determination of
whether or not to help others is an
important, imperative, personal

decision in life. I wonder at what blind hell I would be crawling the floors of today, hadn't my instructors led me properly astray over the years.

It's also important to remember, regarding out-of-order organizational leadership, that leaders awry are not leaders actually. These contradictory agents, notwithstanding the philosophical zombie hypothesis, do manifest in bad faith and often some response is required. It can even be said that derelict agents are innocent victims of so-called original sin, assuming that everyone is OK at their very heart at least for beginnings. Admittedly, it is challenging to maintain that asymptotic perspective, so it's generally always left up to the professionals.

Speaking from experience I say, good can be removed from a person entirely. Everybody starts out with goodness, but it can be lost completely, irrespective of how so. It's never too late to mend, given proper time.

A key to any black magic is its collusion with natural law, as is the case with traditional mob rule or other active bad faith agency among communities. Along these lines come questions of community management. If a person is beyond redemption in this life, and so is endangering the peace, then options include intervention and corrective action. Someone with a line on the situation and the capability to intervene is obligated by rights.

Beyond a certain crossroads of one's education as an individualist, no further instructions are taught for how exactly to move forward. There may be plenty of suggestions in the marketplace of ideas but the guidelines are abstract, merit-based folkways.

It's my observation that all people, eventually, get exactly what they have coming to them. The sword cuts every way. These words describe, briefly, the contents of my mind as I told my new friend Jules that I kill people. The statement invites explanation, or it should, it's meant to. Philosophically, any malefactor can be repaired without actually being made physically dead. But even when apparently neutralized, they may continue to pose real unforeseen threats to others, thus bringing to bear the ethics of helping ungrateful people.

sixty-five.

These days, progressive or experimental social policy can involve personalized world building, with a tragic loophole that gives leave for

demagogues to rule as the tyrants
they've ever evolved to be. That's
fundamental biological reduction.
Their constituencies, upon identifying
the situation and finding out, can walk
away from the bondage as a legitimate
and well-advised postmodern choice.
But a major ethical problem occurs
where souls are caught in the gravity
of the actual living hells created by
fishtank despots. It also brings a
more universal problem, represented by
trolls under bridges in such fish tanks
that unsuspecting people may happen
across in social commons.

Ideally, everyone with proper
cause gets to wear a funny hat because
one does as one must ultimately.
There's no encumbrance for action
executed properly by rights, whether
for one's own sake or others'. That's
the nature of diligent due process.
So, for me it should be an exercise
strictly academic when I duck into some

fish tank for purposes strictly
business. It shouldn't surprise me, it
shouldn't get under my skin.

Why is a particular individual
being given a chance to mend? Time is
the answer. Such operators are given
what time they may have. It's a gift
from those who abstain from responding
to a personal transgression, in order
to make way for karmic law, for better
or for worse. It's an optimistic
gesture because, truly, it's never too
late to mend. Yet, foolishly often
such a gift is not taken advantage of
sufficiently.

It's also a bother when an
offending fishtank despot remains at
large; for example in this instance,
you weren't there to fix it but I was.
And I left that particular mogul in
office, at the peril of the greater
community and the cost of my own
exposure to liability for failing to

resolve the matter when I had the
chance.

Loose ends. Forgotten land mines.
In this instance, for the personal
offense, I gave the gift of time. I
pulled myself off the case and let it
ride on faith in my own astrology, but
I did so at the calculated cost of
exposing everyone to my own interim
risk. Comeuppance is narrowly
tailored, qui facit per alium facit per
se, but the universe is a philosophical
creature and there can be fish tanks
anywhere. Anywhere one goes, there's a
risk of being ciphered as chattel.

A fishtank braintrust ranges from
complex to about one step removed from
elemental motion. For example, the
people who lived by the laundry room at
my old apartments in Phoenix. Although
they appeared to have been drunk and
dying, they exercised squatter's rights
for the purpose of shaking down the

laundry coin boxes. They were like
mean little coin-operated laundry
robots fueled by cheap handles of
whiskey, and cigarettes.

My point is that this mutation
away from peaceable coexistence belies
the influence of something far from
egalitarian. Laundry despots are just
one of the problems encountered in such
fish tanks, for which main drags
include the demand for cheap handles of
whiskey in my voting precinct and the
hard sell that caste lodging in
stairwells is a tractable lifestyle.
Oh, me, I'm sounding like a politician.
Maybe that was the correct answer for
Jules, instead of "I kill people." Or
maybe I'd just rather kill people than
be a politician.

The guy at the end of the bar
left, but I didn't see him pay. He
must have a tab, I thought.

"This is pretty good soup." I had
eaten it all, and all the crackers too.
"I'll be back for more tomorrow,
unless...uhh...when's your shift over?"

"Six."

"Shall we take in a film? In
addition to being a charitable asshole,
I'm a privileged elitist."

"You're probably a taxpayer too."
She reached below the bar, pulled out a
newspaper, and handed it to me.
"Cinema, yes. Suggest a title?"

I could hear the cook's radio
through the kitchen door as I watched
Jules do closing duties. I thought of
taking a short walk to kill the time,
then thought better, since it was
already five-thirty.

Mine in those days was the
standard lot of an individualist. The

situation wasn't bad although it had
taken time and effort to achieve. Time
is of the essence, as nature
accommodates infinite contemplation for
anyone with a will to pause and think
of what life is, or to attempt broad
assessments in order to do right by the
universe.

    We left at six-thirty. Two
waiters relieved Jules in anticipation
of increased demand for floor staff on
the evening shift. She threw her black
book and apron into the back seat of my
sedan, we got in, and I steered us
toward the university district in Tempe
for some art house cinema. Two hours
later we emerged from the theater into
the warm summer night air.

    It was the middle of August.

sixty-four.

"Let's keep ourselves pleasantly occupied, if you're not in a hurry to get home." I said.

"Fine." she said. "Keep it clean and above the belt."

It was nearing ten and I was grateful for the night's occlusion of the desert sun. We drove north to a Phoenix bistro where I was inclined for tea and noodles. Jules had green tea soup.

"Where are you from?" I asked.

"What's a good response to something like that? I'll answer, it's no problem, but let me think about it first." She smiled back. She didn't have crocodile eyes. At a glance she looked like, well, like every woman, in a good way. I could tell she was thinking seriously of the best way to answer my question.

Denver Day

     In terms of looks, down here in
this sideways world, so many people are
covered with war paint regardless of
their gender, and when it comes to
individuals, the when of looking at
them is frequently more relevant than
the who. But female agency is
important, and of a kind. In large
part, I am the way I am because of
women. It's nothing which I would
assign blame for, although it did hurt
like a motherfucker and has taken four
decades (so far). But pain is a small
price to pay for vision and autonomy
and time as an investment gives
excellent kickbacks.

     "Where am I from? Part of the
answer is to say that you and I are
related. Everyone is. It's part of
the human condition. We're all related
to trees too, and even rocks. And
we're Americans so we're essentially
from the same town, Ricky. Just look

at this joint we're in now, and does it seem familiar? Don't get me wrong, I ain't complaining. But I am your girl next door from Texas. That's it. I'm D.I.Y., I came out of no fucking box, and here we are, brother."

"I feel lucky to have such a neighbor. Welcome home in Phoenix. ¿Y yo? I spent the past ten years on I-10 as a Florida-based logistician, and came back here last year to close on some family business."

"Lo te siga." she said. "As with most anyone, my ongoing presence can be described as a function of survival. I'm an accumulation of statistically successful efforts at stop-loss, dead reckoning, and long trains running. If one has one's shit orderly enough for effective evasive action, there's usually enough gray matter left intact to accommodate the psychology of living."

Denver Day

"Talk to me about night and day, Tex. Do you believe all this bullshit about the sun rising and setting?"

"It's a pack of lies." She pulled a deck of cards from her bag, and shuffled them. "And a farce not nearly as old as it would like to be. Anyway, it's horse latitudes for me now. Don't you be a prick or a fucking maniac, Trucker Rick. You just be real cool and patient, and kind, and helpful, and the like, and you will find me to be useful in your world." She winked and farted. Horse latitudes indeed.

Nobody who's anybody smokes anymore, or drinks either. Not at my age. Like she said, it's a survival thing. Or a survivor thing. She dealt me a common hand while discreetly ogling two women who used the door, and came to some judgment about them before returning her attention to our table;

Such pro bono police work is easy to come by and it matches wilderness camping in its efficacy for killing time. I beat her with a hand of three threes.

"I ought to check on my roommates. You're welcome to come and meet everyone. You may sleep on the couch if you'd like."

I accepted. "Rolling stones gather no moss. Does your restaurant need a part timer?"

She laughed. "I know that's funny. I'll check. Otherwise, you can run errands for me and I'll tip you out myself."

sixty-three.

It wasn't a long drive to Jules' suburban residence in north Phoenix.

Denver Day

The south side would've raised an
eyebrow; South Mountain itself is a
natural barrier at least for purposes
of urban motoring, and to go around it
is to leave Phoenix. One of the
interesting things about urban
management in the high desert is that
people could be regularly eating people
at the next mountain over, and no alien
would ever be the wiser. But
historically that seems to have been
the nature of criminal justice anyway.

     Over-educated restaurateur types
like Jules don't live in places like
South Phoenix. Maybe it isn't bad down
there, but it could be interpreted as
bad-looking in some ways. Such is the
aesthetic where metro downtown
districts abut the edges and seams of
older civil infrastructure. Houston's
Fifth Ward comes to mind, for example.

     In fact, I ended up south of
downtown last week when I missed a turn

to the Maricopa County Recorder's
Office. South of the Diamondbacks'
stadium, there are still a few old
houses with working porch lights but by
and large, south of downtown by north
of South Mountain looks like a dock
setting that's been cleared to film a
Miami Vice warehouse explosion. The
area is a slippery concrete slope with
little cover and no green and only the
most obvious of places for a shooter to
hide, unlike most of the post-
industrial United States' llantera-
covered sprawl that contains abundant
nooks and crannies to provide cover for
unelectable snipers. Talk about eating
people.

Her neck of the woods was
reasonably close to my own apartment
off Highway 51. A difference between
me and Jules was that I had, long ago
during my drinking days, alienated all
of my "friends." Down to zero. It
follows that after a person loses the

Denver Day

very last friend, there are no longer
"two sticks" so to speak, for rubbing
together to make new ones. It's funny
how common human relations work that
way, or at least they did for me.
Anyway the point is that I didn't have
a house full of roommates like Jules.
Not anymore and not again yet.

I do have an incidental community
of "friendly" or sympathetic people,
ad hoc. My partisans, more or less.
Cops, bondsmen, activists, artists,
spooks, geeks, honest politicians,
professors, and just general people
I've met in the professional realm.
They're other people with whom I happen
to share vocational space. It's a good
crowd, truth be told, although they're
strictly business, inasmuch as life is
work. A no-nonsense attitude is
important as we ride the high seas of
the universe; someone has to be the
fucking straight guy, and there aren't
many. The whole population cannot be

on shore leave or the world gets
scuttled. It happens to universes all
of the time; everybody wakes up, and
the chickens are in charge, and the
rats across town are back-dooring you
and yours.

This line of work is honester,
anyway. Maybe I could be dwelling in a
cube, plotting to screw the new dish at
lunch hour, playing tennis with fish
brains, wiping my ass with large bills,
hadn't I burned those bridges with
extreme prejudice. There has not been
any extra nepotism left for me, not for
many years, even before I figured out
that the establishment is slavery. But
there's no avarice either, and I'm
thankful for being relatively free of
it all.

Although I sure did get treated
like shit before coming to my stark
realizations about class and labor. I
was not one of them, so I was the hated

other one. There is no middle of the
flock. I wonder, for how many
generations my legacy will last, before
or if someone in my family tree
forgets, doesn't know, or doesn't care
and pulls eighty years as a picture-
perfect secular businessperson before
turning to stone. Even at my final
cube, the company man still had to fire
me, and even then, I granted him the
satisfaction of witnessing my earnest
protest.

We parked and went walking up to
her condo, which was bustling. The
scene felt like an open-all-night
office, not unlike my home workspace,
though Jules' was more heavily staffed.
Comfortable electricity wet the quiet
air. I was seated on the couch, and
someone brought me hummus and mineral
water from the kitchen. A late edition
of the local news was on the television
set. Here and there, a roommate gave a
nod, wave, or walk-by.

sixty-two.

"We're actual people. Not students in the corporate sense but we try to mind the store." she said. "I only tentatively self-identify as "people" since most probably can't be categorized as sentient. Beyond the mean intelligence of their venereal diseases, with chance and luck being what they are, most are probably philosophical zombies by your own estimation. Nevertheless, as a disguise, feigned stupidity is unoriginal and heavily overused."

"And what about people like us?" I said. "For example, there is no more fucking for me, for years now. It is mostly intentional though it's not my first preference. Despite all of my clawing at my own fetters, I created this circumstance knowingly. I'm an

ace, a postmodern monastic, walking a
thin line for strangers who can't
appreciate, or don't understand,
altruism."

"Ironically, sex is good for us."
she said.

"It's one of the few and simple
keys to living." I said. "Yet, some
abstain in the present so others won't
have to figure it out on their own. My
situation is a kind of bondage, there's
no doubt."

"Think of it as a dharma problem."
she said. "The past is a reflection
and the future is conjecture, one's a
thought and the other an idea, and both
are philosophically contingent upon the
existence of a present moment where the
future and past literally and
philosophically shall not exist. And
since various minds define perfection
differently, some avoid certain

vanities for the sake of philosophical perfection. Asceticism, it's a form of austerity, a sacrifice where hegemony is sought at a depth beyond what most fathom to obtain. Such projects don't have to be mutually exclusive of sexuality or sex, but, sex as a distraction leads many people directly away from enlightenment. In that sense, sex can be as deadly as avarice."

"So I've erred on the side of caution." I said. "For the sake of some conjectural future aesthetic, at the risk of its historical irrelevance. There is much that can go wrong. With lovers, I don't believe I ever did anything right, but experience teaches me that friendship is what's most important. I define "friend" differently than I used to, and differently than most seem to. As for people like us generally, or me and you specifically, yes it's a dance with perfection but not at the peril of amity. The romantic muse isn't spooky or shallow and we probably won't fuck this up. Not in a bad way."

"It's no big deal, right? News of the world is news to many." she said. "But since education is entropic, we could still end up on the nine o'clock news wearing only handcuffs and underwear, regardless of our state of enlightenment. Wishing to retain all of its repertoire, corporate media propagandists are disinclined to relinquish any options. No plot of grand tragedy which could effectively invoke posse comitatus, force majeure, martial law, and *1984*-ever comes off the table. Beware that there are too many people who are over-hedged on the eschaton, and that the fifth column's not here to help people with amnesia recovery and divorce counseling. The proletariat won't tell you when the last tree is gone, so it's nobody's job

but ours to prevent the day when only
sick birds, robots, and tire stores
remain. And if it does happen, it's
nobody's fault but mine."

"The fucking robots." I said.
"Wouldn't tell us because they wouldn't
know. Have you been reading my mail?"

"Llantera bots." declared Jules.

"They're fuck bots too." I said.
"Did you ever see *Bladerunner*? There's
more to those Replicants than killing.
Anyway, this world's already ended, or
at least the matter must be prosecuted
as if it had. Notwithstanding men
about horses, there is something very
practical, honest, and quaint about
lovemaking, but in light of the fact
that successfully implemented self
denial opens the gate to greener
pastures of metaphysical being, I've
learned to do without, begrudgingly, to
date. I can also do without all the

herpes, though. Just the other day,
one of the hookers living in my
apartment building fell down the
outside stairs. For any number of
reasons, I'm surprised the woman can
even walk at all, when she can. It
does shine a light regarding where a
progressive lack of mindfulness might
deposit you."

"Do you have herpes?"

"No, not the penis kind." I said.
"I never get cold sores either, but I
don't do much making out anyway."

"Maybe I'll let you kiss my ass
sometime."

"Who is the president?" I asked.

"That depends on what and who you
are. And on what you mean by the
question. Are you talking about the
President of the United States of

America?"

"I don't know. Maybe. But who's the boss of you?"

"The U.S. Executive legally has the oversight of operations, prescribed or incidental, which describe any official executive function of the United States." she said. "Which is most often encountered in our daily life by way of the American dollar. But no, nobody is in charge of me as such, though I do have some creeping existentialist malaise. Yourself?"

"By rights, nobody is qualified, except me." I said. "But I do have ad hoc advisers, like you."

"So you're qualified?" she said.

"Sure." I said. "And may your beard grow ever longer."

Denver Day

"Here's to it." Jules raised her bottle of mineral water.

"Elsewise, do you like to fuck women?" I interrupted, at the risk of disturbing the peace. Evidently, she took no offense.

"As a full-blown adult, the end often turns out that way." she said. "It's a natural option but love's born in the heart, not the crotch."

"There is also safety in numbers, it is said." I said. "It's not a silver bullet but for example, polyamory might resolve certain problems of jealousy, codependency, and other unwanted byproducts of greedy coupling. Due to the non-dualistic nature of philosophical truth, unenlightened humanity suffers duality poorly and the cosmology deals harshly with such failure."

"So what are you telling me,
brother? Are we Mack the fucking
Knife?"

"I think that's probably part of
what we are, if we're anything at all.
Can you make mineral water come out of
your nose?"

"Yes. What of it?"

"Sending the right message is
important in applied taxonomy, despite
veracity's tendency for subjective
drift. To understand the truth and to
speak it, we're equally obligated." I
said. "Truth is truth, it's simply
put. But running afoul of organic
complexities is unavoidable when truth
is contested. My or your being Caveman
the Brick might be a disposition that's
honest, but it doesn't mean one gets,
or even deserves any action whatever."

"Every transaction has a sell side

and a back side." she said. "Wedlock, for example. It's a practical civil institution, but by rights of common law, marriage can be interpreted as "animal coupling" or "people one has slept with" which are institutional polygamy in effect. One eats to live and people are fairly liberal when it comes to survival, yes. But, bonding is bonding, no matter how long ago it happened and regardless of politics and talk, historical facts are what they are."

sixty-one.

Jules hopped up from the couch, went into the hall, and returned a minute later with a set of Bugs Bunny pajamas for me to wear.

"Does he sleep with a rattle too?" Someone down the hall yelled.

"Shut up back there nigga, our guest is a charitable asshole, privileged elitist, and blue testicled shaman."

"Watch your fucking language." Came the reply. "And recalling our wager about the N-word, you owe me five dollars."

Such was the way of the gun at their house. I took a quick shower, slipped into the thoughtfully provided pajamas, and came to rest on a couch in the den.

"I've had it. I'm going to bed." she said. It was homey in there and I slept like a rock although my dreams were weird.

Next morning, the household resumed its action at a reasonable eight o'clock hour. For people with non-traditional schedules, eight in the

morning is a wonderful first effort, I
say. Get it correct in your head, just
because people like us keep funny hours
doesn't mean we're layabouts. I walked
into the kitchen and leaned against the
counter.

"We're all vegan, would you care
for a tofu scramble?" she asked.

"Yes. Did you dream well?"

"I always do with a stranger in
the house." she said. "I'm due for a
shift at twelve-thirty, we can chill at
the coffee shop until then in the
fellowship of other existentialist
coogs."

"Got any brass knuckles?" I
asked.

"Maybe, I dunno. I'll check after
we eat."

After our high-protein morning meal we went downtown to a coffee shop which was thick with shoaling bohemes. Humanity. We were birds of a feather in a flock of geeks.

"I like joints like this because I can blend in and feel normal." I said.

"Well happy birthday then." Jules said. "With my having statisticized the secular, it doesn't matter to me where I go exactly, as long as certain minimum standards are met. I've done all the time I'm willing to do as a dishwasher."

"A classic description of the infinite chasm between labor and management." I said. "You are an excellent cook, however."

"But vegan only. I moved up in the kitchen, not out."

Denver Day

Like it or not, say what you will,
someone was burning hashish up at the
coffee bar. It follows that everyone
in the room, if they're like me, would
be secondhand stoned for the next three
days. I'm like an old retired hippie,
walking a straightedged line in the
modern era, and I'll always prefer
ambient black chocolate to secondhand
corporate tobacco smoke, regardless of
the current decade.

Meanwhile, outside, a houseless
person was being put into the back seat
of a police car.

sixty.

The individual in the back of the
cop cruiser wasn't any of the young,
lurid, addiction-bedraggled stereotypes
seen about various highway junctions.
He was an owl of a person who,
regardless of any shortcomings had made

the less than minor effort of growing a
beautifully kept beard, thick and long
and marvelously flowing. The true
urban bear whose presence is actionable
political speech, a vote of no
confidence in the society that's the
subject of his rejection. The station
they mind is no joke. Just ask someone
who's been around for a while; their
existence belies a personal philosophy
of a deeper fathom, and a very
widespread one, historically.
Naturalism of this sort (whose
signature is invariably accommodated by
aestheticians) is firmly vested in the
marketplace of ideas. Such are
mountains, aesthetically and
politically.

When the standard bearers of
natural law come to bad ends at the
velvet or dead hands of automata, the
convictions of their movement are
compounded in spades. This is a
conversation about social construction

and the nature of organic humanity.
The philosophy, numbers, and political
will of naturalists are strong, and the
ad hoc constituency is known for its
ability to sacrifice, for the sake of
principle and long-term action, far
beyond what most institutions compel
from their adherents. Reasons being
for such tenacity include the
authenticity and the karma of deep
ecology's political incumbency.

"I'll be right back." Jules said,
standing, and walked outside to parlay
with the uniformed officer. She
returned to the table after a one-
minute conversation.

"That's a date." she reported
back. "Those two parties are
acquainted and the man is not under
arrest or duress. It's a public
transport courtesy of the taxpayers of
Maricopa County, to deescalate a
situation with some third party around

here who we've apparently missed.
T'were a civil issue and no more."

"Politics." I suggested.

"People have opinions." she said.

"And the uniform?"

"A young man. Very young
actually, probably in his early
twenties, doing his part, riding a
metal horse."

The barista behind the bar, a
woman with a shaved head, was
overhearing our conversation. "That
guy pisses on the porch out there.
Regularly." she said.

"During business hours?" Jules
asked her.

"Sometimes. Typically only when
it's dark, and no precipitation today.

Paying customers can be just as bad
though." she said, with a faintly
detectable air of condescension, and
went back to her bar dishes.

    "I don't know if that's a proper
hipster attitude coming out of that
barista or not." Jules said. "Then
again, what isn't."

    "It's probably some things but not
other things, and everything's its own
special case." I said. "Whether
baristas or urban owls or reasonably
priced road hazards like us. Shall we
make out in the bathroom?"

    "*I Ching* so." Jules replied. We
ambled together back to the lavatory.
In Phoenix, one often encounters gender
non-specific public toilets, which
evoke an applied, peer-reviewed honor
system that results in more mindful
public toilet use. The honor system.
My friend backed up against the sink

and we enjoyed five minutes of sloppy kissing, groping, and mild dry-humping. We got pretty worked up for thirty-somethings before returning to the bar with horns aglow.

fifty-nine.

Back to our seats, Jules put a ten dollar bill on the bar and set an empty teacup on top of it, glanced at the front door, and gave me a funny look.

"You can either watch or you can go wait in the car because in a few moments we'll be leaving here in a hurry." she said.

Instinctively, my brains went into unknown-risk-calculation mode, trying to solve the universal question of Jules' intent. I went and stood by the door, warily. It turned out that my hasty guess about what she was up to

Denver Day

was accurate.

The barista's somewhat inconsiderate words about "paying customers" were unoriginal but they were hers that morning. It was not clear to me, regarding the person's understanding of the phrase in its fundamental context, or its potential blowback, or what it said of the speaker's attitude about people, baristas, the marketplace at large, and our incidental part in it that morning.

So the first person I'd kissed, in I don't know how many years, mounted her bar stool and took to her knees in a low perch; The lady Jules of Texas looked like a cat about to attack, wanding her narrow rear back and forth capriciously. At first, for a brief moment, I thought she might piss on the bar.

When the unduly self righteous and

soon-to-be-no-longer-uneducated barista passed by that area again, the top half of Jules' body swung back and her right leg made a roundhouse kick over the bar top. The kick connected with the head of the barista, who dropped onto the floor, out cold. Jules moved in my direction, toward the threshold. I reached the car moments before she did, turned the engine over, and we were off.

There had been a thin crowd in the coffee shop, but despite its brutishness, her assault was quick and nearly discreet. People are so generally inattentive that I don't think anyone saw the deed but me. In the eyes of anyone who troubled themselves to look up, Jules could have been running for her life or rushing into the arms of a friend. Alternatively, any witnesses might also know there can be good cause for such an act, easily. I was slightly rattled but no one chased us.

"There are two sides to every story, Tex." Vague apologetica I remarked, respecting my associate's behavior while getting us the hell out of the area.

"We'll be fine as long as we don't go back." she said. "Whether we're paying customers or not."

"What put you over, the wink or the walk?"

"All of it, coming from the wrong demographic, and aggravated by an aversion to wasting the chi from our restroom interlude. Your thoughts?"

"You calculate risk well enough. Maybe the biggest gamble you made involved my reaction."

"I don't think so dude, you're

obvious."

I changed the subject. "Who are those women you live with?"

"Near carbon copies of myself. They are trustworthy people and we get along well."

"Cloning oneself politely, within a most intimate personal community, always presents an interesting challenge. How to lay and hatch one's clutch among the roommates appropriately?" I mused.

"If all else fails, just do it in the butt." she said. "A great zen koan, yes."

My joint didn't offend Jules. Then again, it isn't an offensive place. I packed my gym bag. "Just a precaution Tex. You're a little unpredictable."

"Unpredictability is the nature of things." she said. "There can be no fine control of the helm without a full course of entropy. One must grip it to steer it."

fifty-eight.

We looked at each other as I packed a few things. Jules sat on the couch, making herself at home. We might have screwed like alley cats during those tender moments, riding out the wake of the coffee shop brouhaha, but we didn't. Lest we be forever behind the eight ball, we were cautious not to rest on our laurels.

In the toilet, that was different. For one, it was in the toilet, which is usually reason enough. Two, it precipitated a swift, violent citizen's adjudication. The former impulse act

was fair enough to satisfy local rules,
and a first kiss usually stirs up
enough dust to light some sort of fire.
Jules' subsequent election for natural
justice definitely made a three-bagger
of our morning, but there was still a
risk of cashing in prematurely on the
karma. Religion calls it superstition,
necromancers say common sense, others
see it as standard law of the sea;
Regardless of our epistemological
perspective, Jules and I couldn't
afford to be coasting down the real
highway of sex and justice without
paying proper dues. No one's credit is
good enough for a free ride, not for
long, so before further transacting
with the hegemons of sex and death, we
would need to buffer our account.

Historically, it was a sensitive
moment in my apartment actually, which
if mishandled would have meant a
terminal decline in our greenfield
friendship. But we knew better, and

entered a tacit agreement that gave us
a metaphysical sustainability instead.
As this story continues to unfold, it
should become clearer to you just
exactly what I mean by that.

"Nice little apartment. What's
the management like?" she asked.

"When I renewed the lease, the
rent went up twenty dollars." I said.
"That's what happens when one offers
good faith political will and in-kind
equity to a community that serves no
ends except stupidity, vice, and death.
I did ask why the price went up, and
got a one-word quote for an answer:
"Management." Right out of the horse's
mouth. But if I'm the only "paying
customer," rent must be an unavoidable
cost for me."

"It could be that she feels
shortchanged, you know, when she's the
only one collecting rent but you're the

only one paying it."

"In other news someone, the fabled
"management" perhaps, has stocked a
new mysterious upstairs hooker,
following the eviction of the previous.
Meanwhile two weeks ago, as two dudes
made an overly aggressive pickup of the
one in the building across, I thought I
might have to conduct a shotgun wedding
on that staircase. I telephoned the
sheriff's office but only reached an
answering machine. Next time, if I
really have a care, I'll know to run my
own detail. These women are my
neighbors and I do have various odd
conversations with them, but I don't
really offer the sort of input they're
seeking, generally."

"I support you a hundred-and-ten
percent." she said, changing the
subject. "Now, about what you'll wear
to work. I suggest a nice pair of
black or dark blue jeans, and something

Denver Day

similar along those lines up top, maybe
a golf shirt or a clean, pressed t-
shirt. You're a generalist and I'll
put you in my tip pool. You can expect
anything from dish washing to
bookkeeping, bar backing, or public
speaking."

"That sounds fair."

"Anyway remember, your apartment
manager is probably just following
orders. Compartmentalization of power
and all. You know, respondeat
superior."

"Bullshit." said I. "But I count
myself lucky by life station. Those
who profit from inegalitarian access to
shelter are insidiously criminal and
meaner than both piss-happy philosopher
bums and spurned hookers. This planet
is such a fucking zoo."

fifty-seven.

At lunchtime we got to my new job and relieved the two morning shifters. The pedigree of the clientèle set the bar for urban posh, American suffrage that naturally regulated the crowd size. I washed my hands, scanned the kitchen, and tied on a black apron. Stuck to one of several fridges in the kitchen was a duty list naming local routines for back-of-the-house tasks. Chores for the current hour involved prep work like cutting vegetables to restock the makeline, keeping up with the dishes, and attending short orders that came in from the bar. Pinning down a stack of scribbled recipes upon one of several shelves, I found a little radio covered in a layer of finely accumulated food particles. I switched it on and began chopping onions.

"This domestic pastoral scene will

carry on until five or six, or seven,
or whenever someone relieves us. If
you ever must, when a shift change is
due but nobody's relieved you, wait
some half an hour and then lock up, but
let me know." she said.

That early August afternoon, the
patrons included a dude with big
glasses and a shaved head who was
hammering away at a portable manual
typewriter; two young women each
wearing large headphones jacked into
the same portable audio device; a
table full of relatively youthful
skateboarders; and, seated at the bar,
two black men whose second round of
vegan juevos rancheros was my first
order to fill.

"You need anything, Tex?" I
asked, poking my head through the
kitchen door into the bar area.

"Green tea."

The kitchen's back door led to a typical kitchen outback scene. There was a commercial sized garbage receptacle and a lockable storage shed featuring additional cold storage where I stowed some of my prep work before I left, to wit, five gallons of tomato bisque, five gallons of lentil soup, and five gallons of coconut ginger soup. Et cetera.

That afternoon, I and Jules went through four pots of green tea. Come six o'clock, relief arrived for the kitchen and the front end. She took a few minutes to chat them up, then we walked out to my car and leaned up against it for a few minutes before leaving. She handed me two hundred dollars in cash.

"Not bad for six hours." she said. "Power of the purse and all."

Denver Day

"Let's take a jog and a shower, before we decide how to spend our dark hours."

"That's one way to solve the looming exercise question." she said. "Can you dance?"

"I do alright. Where can we shower?"

"Which of ours is closest, I suppose that's mine."

Since our introduction twenty-four hours before, Jules' roommates didn't seem to have moved or even changed tasks, much less had they changed clothes or work stations excepting some minor lateral movement I'd observed that morning.

"You two assholes don't have much to say." greeted one of her roommates, not the woman named Queenie but the one

80

named Stevie.   "What's your plan?
Reason I ask being, you're part of the
family now, apparently."

"I am many things, like I'm a
writer for example, so I appreciate
your household's operating like an
office."

"Poor work ethic occurs at the
great peril of all good people."
Stevie said, with a smile polite for my
trouble.

fifty-six.

We took a leisurely forty-five
minute run of five miles along a large,
well known local canal frequented by
cyclists and joggers at all hours. We
returned to Jules' condo to shower off
the day's collection of food service
sediment, of which the complete removal
isn't possible in just one wash. That

Denver Day

we can know our peers and competitors
by smell is an old secret among
restaurateurs.

    "I like to dance but the
possibilities of our actually doing the
world some good from a dance floor
tonight are too random and
unpredictable." she said, as she
toweled off her small, delicious
knockers. "It's fun and great exercise
but I think we're better appropriated
elsewhere."

    "It's an odd challenge to be
hunting actively for a "paradigm
shift" when they have a tendency to
arrive in their own good time, and
people trying to "immanentize the
eschaton" are generally agents in bad
faith. It comes down to a difference
in philosophical perspective." I said.
"I'm fairly unsuspecting by nature.
Hell, I remember when someone had to
explain to me the nuances of lying. I

simply didn't recognize or understand it. The reason being for my befuddlement was that, if I know the person's lying and the person knows I know, the jig's up and no further argument can be pressed. Yet the debate was forced beyond logic. I get it now, I was being hustled. I didn't think like a criminal, and historically it made me an easier mark for hustlers. I have learned much, though still I have difficulty reckoning with the rationales for bad faith agency. My being strongly wired for veracity is connected to my drive for survival."

"In lay-person's terms, we're straight shooters, not hustlers." Jules said.

"It's an important distinction yes." I said. "I even once put the question regarding this phenomenon to a colleague. The answer I got was, that subterfuge and obfuscation are the

fancy words for those particular kinds
of lies. These days, I try to be more
guarded, and I try to deal with "other
people" using a more case-by-case
approach. Anyway, is there some place
we can play cards, since we ain't going
dancing?"

   "Besides right here at home, or at
the collective or the coffee shop, we
could go to an actual casino." she
said. "Those dealers aren't bad cops.
We can go north on 87 and be there
within an hour, if you don't mind
driving."

   So was formed our evening plan.
We drove east for a stretch. Roadsigns
marked our entry into reservation
territory, twenty minutes after the
highway bent north whereof our
destination awaited. The Salt River
Casino.

   "It may sound ironic to some, and

many don't realize it, but these reservations preserve American ideals effectively." she said. "Progressive encroachment upon natural liberties in the United States and a cottage industry of bureaucratic government have done things to our nation to make it unrecognizable in many terrible ways. Thankfully, the Native Americans take their citizenship very seriously. Such is constitutional law."

"Following life's more notable comeuppances, one of the tasks remaining in the quick is to preserve the good of what's left, if there's anything left at all, meanwhile dispatching unchecked hazards." I said. "In my experience, the proper tools for these challenges arrive with the accumulation of merit."

"Maybe that explains why things are different on this Native American nation. It's not because the people here are doing things wrongly, if you follow me." Jules said. "The common ground isn't all picture perfect. But compared to other American rights of way, there are remarkable contrasts and similarities."

fifty-five.

We arrived at nine, parked the car and walked into the casino. The floor wasn't crowded although the venue was active enough to buzz properly. Here and there on the porches, we saw live music acts and, well it was nice. Casinos are kind of homey, you know. One might think they'd all reek of avarice, ruin, and desolation based on some dystopian perspective of economics and morality. But, when done correctly they're not, and I think here's the reason why:

Generally, people who understand

the context of their life in the U.S.A. or as free individuals anywhere, understand that paper money is materially worthless, that it's value and usefulness is strictly a matter of its symbolizing guaranty. People come to casinos like this for the same kinds of reasons that Jules and I had. For example, to play cards because it's simply enjoyable to relax and associate with other various folks. There's an engineered timelessness at a casino whose microeconomics is a curiosity except to those for whom it's a traffic stop.

Following a brief restroom break, we bought into a blackjack dealer for a negligible sum to enjoy the time, conversation, and experience. After twenty minutes, Jules asked for a poker table. The dealer pointed rearward and to the left. "But any table will do."

We rowed the suite river for

Denver Day

ninety minutes before getting restless
and closing our book at the poker
table. We walked around the concourse
and found a table near a jazz quintet
on a low stage. A server enabled our
natural cravings for salads, spicy
fries, and iced green tea, and the
musicians topped the artful bustle of
the scene with a warm, glittering
breeze. At midnight we tipped the
staff and settled the check.

The car was halfway through the
second section of the lot. Jules
walked around to her side as I keyed
the driver door, and I heard some
unseen third party speak unintelligible
words. I glanced up in her direction
to see Jules jump back quickly, so I
went around the car to investigate.
When I came around the trunk, I saw her
reach into her boot and pull a blade
which flashed in the floodlight above
us. She opened the throat of the
person on the ground, set the bloody

device onto the chest, and got in the car which I reversed, slowly. We can discuss whether hers were logical thoughts and rational actions, but I'll testify that her mind was perfectly clear.

"He should've known better." she said. "Let's go to a hotel for a while, then you can drop me off and catch up before work tomorrow."

fifty-four.

In its own right, sex and sexuality comprise a proper language, standalone with their own intrinsic currencies, so de facto economic relationships come to exist between sex and the dollar. That would be fine if various organizations weren't recidivist transgressors in the name of religion against natural liberties. For example, sex trafficking is a crime, even when the perpetrator is a church. Religious organizational membership is not exempt from respecting civil liberty. Not even when the religion is a secular governing bureaucracy.

Jules was intent to cash in, if you will, on her latest killing. Her modus operandi was an effort at perfecting her personal agency in departure from the encumbrances of a hyper-sexualized marketplace of commercialized, commodified, and hyper-moralized sex and sexuality.

Sex is the most ubiquitous form of bondage. Other ways of relinquishing freedom are to govern oneself by hearsay, suffer arrogant slander from baristas, or allow undergarment encroachment by alleged assailants in the parking lots of casinos. Following our libidinous act of preservation and advancement of human intellectual and

sexual hegemony, it became clear to me
she meant well by her agency. But
speaking of sex, right or wrong, the
sex act about to happen also situated
me unequivocally to her killing, as a
philosophical accessory after-the-fact.
So I would need faith in Jules' self
mastery, in her avoidance of the
classical forensic snares of the
aforementioned socio-historical
trappings.

On our way back to the metro area,
I pulled into a tidy roadside hotel and
we checked into a downstairs room that
faced the highway. There was no need
to shuck all clothes and I didn't
bother with front door parlay because
we're on a budget and lily gilding
takes the back seat in a bull market.
Someone had left the t.v. set on and
whither commenced the assfucking one
minute later, neither of us bothered to
switch it off.

Denver Day

"Sometimes, there's no time to beat around the bush with toe licking and pussy eating." I said. "Sometimes just the bare facts will do for crucial fluid exchanges, because the universe is just a big asshole. That's one of the sorcerer's stones, you know."

"Thank you Professor Quine. I like your rooster and appreciate your kind donation. Let's hit the road." We left the key at the front desk, that was unoccupied except for a droning television.

"Same shift for both of us tomorrow?" I asked when I dropped her off.

"Yep, come over first thing in the morning. We'll go to breakfast and maybe look for a new girlfriend unless you'd rather a mule."

The time was three in the morning,

the flesh was peacefully exhausted, the
mind was wide awake. Over the years,
I've cultivated a practice that allows
the body to sleep while the mind stays
waking. It's sort of an applied lucid
dreaming mode for overachievers. I
elected not to shower for preserving
the insides of Jules' backside on my
pipe, made a journal entry, then
convalesced guilt free, until nine when
I returned to Jules and company.

fifty-three.

"What keeps us from traveling?"
she said.

"Nothing important." I answered.
"It's late August. We'll save our
money for a month and hit the road.
Any ideas?"

"No. We'll figure something out."

Denver Day

"Is three a crowd?" I asked.

"That depends on situations and personalities." she said. "On our autumn road trip, probably so, at least for starters."

I changed the subject. "Do you come here often?"

She laughed at me. "No, but I did last night. Thank you again, for shoving my asshole like a good daddy should."

"How are your grits?" I stirred my grits.

"Going right through me." she said. "Let's leave by October. Maybe we're back by the yule or maybe we're gone all winter."

"Will work take us back?" I asked. She said it would.

Since we didn't have any particular reason to travel, we had some decisions to make as we planned the satiation of our continental wanderlust and at-large distribution of justice. No extraordinary reason is necessary because this North American continent is a big chunk of land that warrants exploring, and failure to do so is comparable to announcing oneself as a scholar of world religions for having studied none other than one's own.

So we spent the rest of the morning at that table in our diner, pencil sketching the faces of each other and our peers in the room. Drawing strangers is curious. Some people are immediately aware of their audience, some are aloof. Some are evasive or hostile and others pose, knowingly or subconsciously. We returned to Jules' dwelling and spent

Denver Day

ninety minutes preparing for our
afternoon shift at the collective. The
household displayed its trademark buzz
of business office snap. Stevie, who
was editing the memoir of some local
hack, asked me if we had a nice time at
the casino. I still hadn't directly
engaged the other woman, Queenie, whose
nook was better hidden from the commons
of their dwelling.

"Was good. In other news, we're
taking a road trip of unknown duration.
What about you? You're dedicated, but
I wonder what else you do?"

"Maybe do you mean, "can I fuck
your asshole too, Stevie?"" she said.

Oh dear, I thought, I'm not sure
what it is, but here it comes....

"I can tell you." she added.
"The answer is "probably" but you'll
have to earn it."

I didn't know whether I'd won or lost. "That's all? What are you, some kind of capitalist?" I asked.

"No. Shit no brother, I'm giving it away but my asshole is inextricable from its actual value." she said. "My bottom isn't a fiat currency."

"Hmmm. That sounds like more of a transaction than an agreement."

"Any agreement is a transaction, philosophically." she said. "And the marketplace of ideas is a real ontological thing whose constituency includes you and me and my asshole, and real interactions involving gravity and heat and such. It's the nature of things both strong and weak, Rick the Rooster, quid pro quo. Meta economics is complex."

"Are you describing the karma or

the dharma?" I asked.

"Both, but don't confuse one for the other."

"All dharma is fire." Jules watched me pour some tea for Stevie, and the rest in a cup to go, then off we went to the collective.

Give or take a few deviants, the crowd was a facsimile of the lunch crowd from the day before. I made a big pot of actual green tea and, pondering our travel options, we began our afternoon of quaint Americana. I found some pie recipes, sharpened the knives, cut more vegetables to freshen the line, and knocked out the dishes from the previous shift.

fifty-two.

September was relatively

unremarkable, as we saved our scratch
and prepared for the road trip.
Everyday is not Halloween, if only in a
very limited number of ways, so we
continued our daily duties diligently,
letting our vacation come to us.

We took our leave of Phoenix in
the small hours of the first Monday in
October. On the way out, I dropped off
paperwork at the federal courthouse
west of downtown. Then we drove to the
nearby Maricopa County Recorder's
Office and then the state house, at
each of which Jules left a sealed
envelope.

"Nothing beats some fuckin'
nationwide sightseein' mama." she
said. "Northward, shall we?"

North? Why not. Without fateful
choices, we're actually sightseeing not
traveling, no? This continent is full
of space-aged roads, gasoline, and

vehicles, yes, but one's relationship with the scenery can vary. In the States, there is a huge and important transient demographic of whose ranks Jules and I just then joined as a duo, temporarily as far as we knew. The continent's honeycombed lattice of overland highways enhances and expedites the free assembly which, for so many people is more than enough for a permanent mission.

"Motorcycles are more ecological and natural." I said. "What's your business at the recorder's office?"

"I'm trying to get a feel for the local taxation racket, what a scam. Sniffing around to discover the bridge trolls around here these days. Oh, and bikes are nice but we can't sleep in them if necessary."

"Oh. The fucking mob in government is a bigger problem in the

U.S. than many people realize." I said. "It's so bad, people don't understand they don't have to listen to criminals. Like, just because sex workers have rights and of course they do, doesn't mean they're definitively in charge of the Federal Reserve Bank. In the afterlife, tax protesters get merit honors and shiny badges. Maybe the only honest aspect of the cottage industry of usury exists among a slim portion of its honest bondsmen. Meanwhile ex-convicts may be the only honest politicians. Do you own any real property?"

"Mmhm a very little." she said.

"What about the errand at the state house? Submitting legislation?" I asked.

"Yes, in fact. Basically, my abridged political manifesto. As far as I'm concerned, it's properly lodged when any paid civil servant reads it." she continued. "Hey by the way, what's the capital of Utah?"

"It may be fortuitous that you brought your briefcase as we are en route for Salt Lake City." I said.

"I left my public affairs in Phoenix." she said. "What about your business at the courthouse?"

"Providing some information about crimes."

"Crimes such as?"

"Those typically deriving from standard human failings like fraud, misappropriation of the public trust, theft by paper tools. Cockroaches and the like." I said. "Offenders vary by name but rarely stand out in stripe."

"And they rarely knock. It ain't

nothing nice." she said. Clear of
conscience and trouble, we stayed our
bearing northerly, enjoying views of
desert and mountains.

fifty-one.

This new colonial city is an
interesting confluence of dedicated
civil infrastructure, exemplary rugged
individualism, and the carpetbaggers
borne invariously of a remotely located
regional seat of government.

Salt Lake City is hidden in plain
sight geographically, stowed amid the
ponent continental expanses of the
Rockies. With all deliberate speed,
its suburban pedigree porters the
impressive cargo of the mormon
prophet's neoapocalyptic twenty-first
century legacy birthright. Market-
wise, it's an industrial banking hub
and that'll be a financial commendation

probably retained even if the city becomes suddenly much closer to sea level. In addition to the aforementioned soccer moms, politicos, and industrialists, the city has some lovely artists, like punk bands and dramatists. And admirably odd dram shop laws.

"There's some shift work for us here of the same nature as our collective in Phoenix, and it's probably worth staying here for a few days to take advantage of it." Jules said. We motored thereabout for some tea and company. There was no reason to watch the clock closely, but I think it was nine or ten in the evening. Actual time is an astronomically approximated, organic relativity. Maritime geodesy notwithstanding, a calendar sourcing only a single stellar body, moreover a towering local one, is effective like a furled sail or a laundry line hanging from one pole. A philosophically valid daily clock must start at a point and never end, kind of like military time. Time is fiat property. Albeit easily sworn "all day" is an eternal commitment.

When we came to the local collective, Jules got into a long conversation with some stranger near the door. The main room was large and fairly well occupied with people playing chess, drinking espresso, burning incense and tobaccos, more crowded than our home base. Of several open tables I chose a well-worn wooden one. Despite the international criminal syndicate upon which stands much of the global coffee trade, I considered how the scene was so alive and valuable compared to any based on alcohol. Jules rejoined me in due time with a chess board from a nearby binful of tabletop games.

"I'll set 'em up if you'll go to

the bar and get us some dinner, eh."
she said. Food order pending, ten
minutes later I returned to the table
with a pot of hot green tea.

"What's the weather like? Any new
warrants?" I asked.

"Touristry can be slightly vanilla
sometimes. We'll accept that as easily
as its cascading entropy." she said.
"Also, that woman invited us to stay at
her house, so we don't have to worry
about a hotel."

"Did we get the afternoon shift?"

"Negative, we're on the
graveyard."

"I wouldn't dare complain."

We played a series of chess,
farmed a few nearby tables into our
games, and drank several pots of tea.

Eventually having our fill of caffeine and board games, at one in the morning we walked several doors over to a smaller venue with live music. It was a metal outfit.

    "Wow. Every one of these people, from the rats down to the dishwasher tonight will keep their heads for being incidental to this ad hoc study in glorious satanism." she said.

    "You familiar with the metal scene?" I asked.

    "Not intensively, but their dedication is admirable."

fifty.

    Nobody drinks anymore. We didn't anyway, but nobody would have known it in that place other than the bartender or maybe the governor of Utah. If it

107

Denver Day

were twice as big, it would have been a
dark, loud, damn crowded small venue,
one easily categorized as a hole-in-
the-wall dive. The long, narrow room
shared the red brick walls of its two
neighbors front to back, on both sides.
Hipster walls, thick with graffiti.
There was a ceiling up there, too.

The metal band was running through
a half stack of Marshall amplifiers.
To be familiar with the technicalities
of such things is to understand, that's
a lot of decibels for a seven-hundred-
square-foot room. The band was
shredding, those amps were cranked, and
the screamer was putting spurs to the
whole cartoon. I admit it was hot and
much too loud for conversation even if
the loudness were halved. Verbal
communication required cupping the hand
and shouting as loudly as possible,
directly into the earhole of the
bartender or whomever. Casual chatting
had to be taken into the toilet or

outside.

Anyway, drinking's not good for one's neural net or firmware and doctors recommend you should stop if you've not already. There were at an intersection of hot audio weaponry, solid state resistors, and organized goat-on-sheepshit heavy metal assembly. The crowd was a mash-up of hipster sociology. Metal crowd is similar to motorcycle crowd, for example the communities deploy rigorous gatekeeping measures, have a good foot forward as a general policy, and are self policing. The personnel overlap at times, of course. It probably wasn't a metal bar strictly, but that night was metal night forever, for sure. We squeezed in at a table of other overgrown up-all-night teenagers and Jules got involved in a screaming, cupped hand to mouth to earhole conversation with the woman next to her. They carried on like that for five minutes.

Denver Day

The band was delightfully guitar heavy, and one of the axes was the type with sharp angles and pointy corners. Unlike hardcore punk rock, some branches of metal have lengthy songs with long bridges and multiple solos. The group's pieces weighed in about ten minutes each, and after three numbers, I got a tap out from Jules. We stood and went out the front door with the woman she'd been earholing.

The air out front was still loud but at least conversationable. Stretching on the sidewalk, we adjusted our jaws, attempting to return the ears to proper function. Jules introduced me to her new acquaintance. The three of us walked to the vehicle and loaded ourselves three deep into the front seat. Man it was nice and quiet, though the ears still rang. The hour was late and I was exhausted, reason being all the day's driving. We had a

healthy sort of tiredness, with Jules
and I still getting our sea legs in
those initial days of the road-trip
adventure. I slept on our host's
couch.

  We got up and went out for
breakfast the next morning, where the
room bustled with human traffic from
Salt Lake City's highways, flyways, and
downtowners. I took a silent
canvassing of the people in the
restaurant, an assortment of others
also eluding moribund wage-slave day
jobs, the insurance racket, official
state religion, murderous corporate
whores, or any number of the other
dirty bastardations that encroach on
free individual will. My pursuit of
the muse marshals honest cause for
ongoing exploration and travel, that's
one of the nice things about this
lifestyle. Such a path only leads to
growth, and even if it gets you killed,
it's a timeless effort in good faith

whose merit transcends the petty
trappings of the profane realm.

If life's being lived correctly,
though, death's not deadly. Dying only
has everything to do with the incorrect
perspectives of others. The muse won't
actually get yourself killed although
people of no faith will be convinced of
such falsehood. To live deliberately
takes a lifetime and truth brings out
the worst in false people. The
lifestyle doesn't have to be tough on
one's mother but it's a full
commitment, so living it can be
challenging, especially if you're a
hard case on a rough ride.

forty-nine.

In an effort to have more command
over my own content, as a writer I
carefully police my subjective
experience or cognitive input. The

practice is advisable regardless of one's station. There is no television at home, so my temporary lodging in hotels and motels or the domiciles of strangers is, for me, always a groundbreaking study in mass media.

Anyway, television eventually steals people's dope. I would say, you know, fuck the telly but I sang a different song before I knew the dangers of the medium for what they are. It's useful to me these days, but more so for non-standard or non-entertainment reasons generally, and notwithstanding the rarity of well-written programming of course. Pro tip: Years of self-imposed media blackouts make it easier to critically assess solicitations and discern hustles; I'm not perfect but it has helped. And aesthetically, television programming is often dismally self-perpetuating and obtusely self-referencing. Done wrongly, it's an

awfully disinteresting pastime that
reminds me of hanging out with drunks,
chain smokers, coke heads, or other
addicts.

So, we turned the set back off.
Yada yada yada "the economy" blah
blah blah "handguns" and "eating
babies" and so on, but not a lick of
critical thought. Most of that shallow
business has been out of fashion for at
least decades although a t.v.
constituency has no idea. Nevertheless
it seems to be little more than a
marketing problem; Worthwhile content
does not sell well.

For lunch we went back to the
local edition of the collective for
smoothies. We hung around downtown
that afternoon, then returned early
evening to our host's address for
additional media scholarship while we
waited for our night shift to come
around. We got to work at nine and I

squared up the kitchen while Jules
dealt cards and counseled the diners
who chose to sit at the bar. Business
was brisk that night and we ended up
walking with two hundred dollars
apiece. Jules' girlfriend showed up at
four.

"I'll meet you at her house in a
couple of hours." Jules said, and they
split wearing all black but without a
stitch of leather. Front-of-the-house
staff relieved me at five thirty. They
were late but I had no cause to
complain. The scene was cool and the
prep work was done. I shot the shit
with one of Jules' friend's people I
recognized from the night before, who
spilled the beans to me regarding new
aspects of my upcoming travel plan. I
finally hit the bricks after ten
minutes of shop talk with my reliever.
Dawn broke. They confirmed the rumor
I'd heard about the next leg of our
journey when they returned home at

Denver Day

eight.

    "We'll be taking her to Austin
after fitting in a few more night
shifts here, then we're driving a load
of shit up to Baltimore."

    "I'd already heard about the Lone
Star State aspect of it." I said.
"Which all sounds fine to me. Are you
looking forward to visiting the realm
of your origin?"

    As I've said, driving allover the
continent for no clear reason had real
value, to me as a writer and a citizen,
or from Jules' point of view as a
painter and a cold blooded killa. Once
we got up there, some associate of an
associate of an associate or so, in
Baltimore down from points northerly,
would be connecting with us for a
contraband swap. That region's a
logistical hub that's not entirely
about friendly fuzzy bunnies. It was

established and is still held tightly
as an independent and extremely
partisan city at an international port.
Like I don't know but I've been told
it's a heroin trafficking hub which is
of interest to me as a former trucker
and because of my studies about the
marketing and other logistical aspects
of black markets.

We worked three more nights and
left Salt Lake City at dark thirty cool
with a purse fatter by eleven or twelve
hundred dollars.

forty-eight.

We drove through the night, made
El Paso by late morning, checked into a
motel, and walked next door to eat.
After brunch we returned to our room,
locked the door and closed the
curtains, took a nice, long a.m.
siesta, and were back on the road again

by nine that evening. We made Austin
by sunrise.

Like Phoenix, Austin is a capital
city and a particularly political
place. At the risk of declaring the
obvious: I say for all the bad rap
imputed to American domestic policy,
the individual state governments avoid
their fair share of impeachment
frequently and probably unduly. By
accommodating local circumspection,
Article Four states' rights to a
republican form of government also
enables local grift. The writ itself
isn't at fault but it's the local
guarantors' betrayal of public trust.
It's all the same to me in the end, but
I'm just saying corruption in public
office alters the constituency and
geography of any racket.

Ancillary to usury, bondage, and
financial coercion, the state agency
derelict is usually the main troll

under the bridge with hammers and
velvet paws although it's been argued
that derelict manifestations of the
I.R.S. are no slouches either. I'm
not making an argument about which is a
lesser evil but mind you, regardless of
who is stealing one's lunch money,
theft and coercion are perfectly
illegal being unconstitutional and a
violation of standard criminal statute.
Anyway, seats of government always have
a certain gilding about them.

Among other various statements,
the political marketing landscape in
Phoenix says fantastic things like
"rugged individualism" and Austin's
boasts of "intergalactic wealth" but
they both have their share of urban
social issues such as homelessness and
sex trafficking, and where right
attitude surfaces, class warfare often
snuffs it. These state systems of
government are imperfect and therefore
aren't philosophically ready for wide-

open capitalization. Ready or not,
however, a devil may care attitude
prevails among rats, and rats do
persevere as a species.

The world's ever-booming black
markets may boom the hardest in big
cities. Usually, any city of notable
size truly has an actual standing army
deployed with a full blown intelligence
operation; a navy is often nice for
providing moral backbone. I'll stop
short of apologizing for turning a road
trip into a study hall for political
science, but this shit is important if
you want to avoid trouble such as
criminals and crime whether
internationally, domestically, or
locally. It can be said that all
politics are local anyway, or speaking
more closely to the vest, all politics
are the same. I realized, as soon as I
learned why we were going to the East
Coast, that the spirit of this lecture
suddenly had everything to do with who

needed to die in Baltimore nevermind Annapolis and I'd never been to either place.

In dreary old south Austin we lodged with a friend of our temporary traveling companion from Salt Lake. After two days and a night we started another twenty-four hour leg of eastbound driving. If I felt there was no reason to get noticed anymore than necessary, by strangers or anyone else, I thought right.

"We are selling dope." she said. "That's our cover story."

"Oh. Is it good dope?"

"Well, it's Austin dope, if that means anything." she said. "Two payloads. One of the nice opportunities about doing a burn in a drug deal is that if it's properly organized, a bad faith politician, public official, or other malfeasant corporate agent gets the business end of the blunderbuss."

"True." I said. "And everyone's a politician but few realize it, some are better at the craft than others but being unaware of one's individual political incumbency is no excuse."

forty-seven.

Twenty-four hours later we stopped in Nashville at a bar called Elvis' Manbird to pick up some materials. The rain persisted as it had since we'd left Austin. Jules went inside and I waited in the car. Five minutes later she returned carrying a garbage bag over her shoulder.

"He also offered firearms and we should probably accept." she said.

"We do have our own."

"Yes and I'd like to keep mine out of the Chesapeake Bay on her vacation." she said.

The instructions to pick up the heaters routed us to an unattended, unlocked vehicle in front of a grocery store a mile up the highway from Elvis' Manbird. In the back seat we found ammunition and four firearms in hardshell cases: a short barreled police issue twelve gauge with a big box of high velocity slugs; a tactical two-forty-three with a loaded jumbo-sized magazine; and two forty-five caliber pistols with a box of hollow points. We put it all in the trunk of my car and began our final approach to Baltimore.

"Looks like we're Baltimore County approved." I said.

Denver Day

"Baltimore's self governing.   An
independent city."   she reminded.

"What exactly are we peddling?"

"The dude back there said it was a
brick of perfect cocaine and a bundle
of diacetylmorphine."   she said.   "It's
supposed to be bait that's large enough
to attract our marks but small enough
to mitigate some of our risk exposure."

"Those are highly subjective
considerations."   I said.

"Suicide, after a fashion, is
weird that way, yes.   All people who
set out to kill themselves on purpose
with heroin usually take a relatively
long time to do it, and there's all
sorts of unavoidable yowling and
suffering during the course of it."
she said.   "The cocaine dance is
different aesthetically, but involves
similar beatings about the bush.   In

124

any case, once attached to its living host, death gets in its own way and taints the quality of life while slowly killing. It takes a lifetime to die. Such creep calls for zen and the art. Anyway it's Mexican Horse and Colombian Blow so who needs Asia."

"The commodity governs without a crown." I said.

"In the morning, I'll initiate our detail with a phone call." Jules said. "Meanwhile let's make a u-turn for an overnight roadside paradise on the westbound side of this vein."

We found one and pulled in under the cover of a cold, dusky, and rainy Tennessee October evening. "We could be done with this deal by lunchtime." I said.

"Right. My call will be a one-way conversation without any bullshit or

waiting for a callback." she said.
"I'll make a second one after we're
done and that's supposed to be it.
From here on out, this will be our
standard operating procedure for our
"citizens' arrests."

forty-six.

That night, despite some natural
jitters and a little travel fatigue, we
enjoyed a sense of steady peace and
clear conscience experienced by those
true to their own hearts, who have
pride in actions which support their
right principles.

So far, Jules and my association
had won us several travel adventures
and new friends, and gotten us laid in
conformance with the political wills of
the hegemons of sex and death. And our
involvement continued to bring about
opportunities for comparably low-risk

domestic civil service, the execution of which would soon conclude all of the heavy lifting for the road trip. Next morning as planned, Jules dialed the contact number. She was on the line less than a minute.

"The deal is, we have two jobs at separate locations. With our political cover and diligent oversight for the usual risks, this should be a piece of cake." she said. "Go-time is in an hour. I'm supposed to call again this evening for the second act."

The cocaine was the first drop, among the quaint suburban sprawl. Our instructions were to bring the gear to the door, knock, be welcomed and enter the domicile, and be cool during the exchange. Then we'd burn down all the buyers, turn on our heels, and exit. I'll grant you, the process doesn't sound subtle. Such things definitely require a certain artfulness.

Denver Day

"We don't know how many there will
be." I said. "The order begins with
whoever actually is looking at us and
anyone clearly armed. We will have the
element of surprise but we won't be out
in the open so anyone hiding in the
back can either stay hidden, or stand
up and take the census."

"Be cool when we walk out and
drive away. That's when we're most
exposed to pot shots or being tailed.
Let's try to keep the rear window."
she said.

"And our fucking heads." I added.

"Mine's itchy anyway. Do you
think it would grow back?"

A car was parked in the driveway,
which was comforting since it provided
some cover for the getaway. Jules put
the coke brick into a paper grocery

128

sack. Our affectation was that of
matronly, non-dangerous visitors who
weren't about to burn someone down in a
drug deal for the purpose of making a
tacit, gratuitous ethical statement
that would probably be unappreciated or
misunderstood by most people. We each
carried one of the complimentary forty-
fives that had been so appreciatively
donated at or near Elvis' Manbird by
anonymous partisans.

I looped around the block to check
for escape obstacles like cul-de-sacs
or dead ends. None were apparent. I
parked at the curb across the street as
to align the car in the driveway
between mine and the door of the house.
Jules grabbed the bag with the cocaine
and we hopped out of the car, leaving
the doors unlocked. On a heavy wooden
front door I gave a shave-and-a-haircut
rap. A man with short salt-and-pepper
colored hair opened up, half a minute
later. He gestured for us to enter,

Denver Day

closed the door behind us, and engaged
us with a smile.

    "I'm Bob. Nice day for delivering
groceries."

    "Hi Bob." said Jules. "Nice
place."

    She stalled a minute to see if
anyone else might come out, but nobody
did. Good and easy, I thought. There
was a bit more small talk, and then
"anyway, here you go." she said,
setting the bag down on a table in the
foyer.

    I reached back, slowly drew the
pistol from its holster, raised the
weapon smoothly and put five rounds
into Bob. Jules added another three
and we left him on the floor, bleeding
out. Shutting the front door behind us
gently, we walked to the car and drove
off.

forty-five.

The shooting took place inside, the gunshots were muffled without, and we encountered no neighbors emerging to investigate. No one jumped out of any cupboards during the job (believe me, we were looking). As we left, there were no other vehicles on the road in the immediate area, and traffic was light all the way back to the hotel.

"I wonder who he was." I said.

"More of a curiosity than a wonder I say. The song remains the same." she said. "What's important is who he'll never be, or who he won't be anymore."

"So the message is what it is, no matter who reads it." I said. "I suppose a nice thing about it not

Denver Day

mattering who actually receives the
message, is we don't have to get
everybody as long as we get somebody.
That may seem obtuse but it suits me.
Do you think there was anyone else in
that house?"

"Oh absolutely shit yes. I can
think it and do." she said.

"Concurring. Some silent witness
wasn't sold on our brown trouser
special of the day." I said. "If
either of us paid enough attention to
the press, maybe we could deduce from
the political agate what organization
just lost a bag man."

"If, indeed." she said. "It's
all the same to me and it's someone
else's job."

We were still holding the heroin
bait and our day's work wasn't
complete, of course. We brunched. We

132

late lunched. We skipped dinner with the intention of eating after the last job, after we were back on the road. Jules made the second call at dusk's consideration.

"They want us over at the East Channel where I-95 ends, to deal with some shitheads under the bridge near Seagirt Marine Terminal." she explained.

"At the risk of wrongly over-generalizing about cocaine dealers having finely manicured lawns and dispositions pacific." I said. "Please keep in mind this is a heroin deal and heroin dealers are shitty people. In fact they're not people, by my standards. What I'm trying to say is these guys may not be as amicable as Bob."

"Fuck 'em all." she said. "So let's go. When we get to the drop,

I'll get out and stand right next to
the door."

By the time we approached the East
Channel, it was full blown nighttime.
She directed me to an exit, a u-turn,
and an idling stop in the turnaround
lane. Two men, a black dude and a
white dude, stood waiting on the
median.

No others made themselves known in
the dim artificial light beneath the
highway. Jules stepped out with the
dope and positioned herself clear of my
fire line. I put a forty-five round
into each of the men's chests and they
both dropped immediately. She drew,
added lead to their heads, and got back
in the car still holding the heroin.

I placed the vehicle into gear and
was completing the turnaround when we
heard gunshots, which I could also hear
connecting with the metal and glass of

our vehicle. I hit the accelerator to
get us around to the westbound feeder.

I could see bullet holes in the
rear glass. She was slumped forward in
the seat and didn't answer. The
vehicle gathered speed as we cleared
the scene.

forty-four.

Fear is a primal thing which can
bedazzle by its sheer surdity. But its
causality can be known. Understanding
the mechanistics of the emotion hinders
its ability to stun, as a mind so
enlightened recognizes irrational
paralysis for what it is. Something as
well as fear surfaces amid tragedy,
however. I've observed a willingness
to transact (with debatable efficacy)
revolutionary, universe changing
decisions when traumatic events are in
the offing. Notwithstanding duress,

such desperate oaths sworn must be carefully chosen, because they can influence one's existence.

I knew the death of Tex was a bellwether for major sea change. Jules' robust spirit was always evident, and her mind and political will were readily accessible to anyone she worked with. Likely due in part to the wearing of her soul on her sleeve, when she died I was encumbered by certain brand new facts. One, I had a new job to do regardless of how I handled the fiasco of the moment. Two, I wasn't alone in my new employment because death doesn't kill the spirit. Certainly not one of such a caliber as hers. Habeas corpus shazaam.

I had learned a previous such lesson, in the parting of a beloved household animal on New Year's Eve 2012, for example. Moses was an indoor/outdoor cat. Night was

approaching and so was a thunderstorm.
He slipped out of the kitchen door, I
didn't mean to let him out, but the cat
will come back when the rain starts
soon, I thought. In short of five
minutes, heavy rain arrived, and it was
likely in those same minutes Mo was
hit, attempting to return before a
soaking. He didn't get right back and
I formed a bad feeling about the
situation. I found the body in the
morning, on a pile of leaves next to
the curb beneath a lamp post and a
large oak tree.

But the night before, when I'd
gone to bed, I felt him jump in with
me, as he did often. He came to say
"well, daddy cat, I lost my body but
I'm still here. I didn't know where
else to go, so I came back home." He's
still with me. For losing himself,
Moses apologized like any good son, and
offered his transcendental
companionship in consolation.

Jules had many partisans and confidantes and intimate associates because she was an open book and a heavily networked woman. But I believe she considered, at the time of her death, some ethical obligation to retain our vocational association if only because its trajectory remained conveniently intact. Alive or dead she understood just as I did, that her political will remained necessary for the continuation of our thriving joint venture.

To stay with me was no skin off her back. After all, I was the one still alive. Recall the dictum, we ought not speak ill of the dead for soon shall we join them or so it will seem, serves at convenience and pleasure beyond the living agency. Jules didn't mind still riding it out with me. In my mind, her continuing patronage was a well-received act of

partnership and dedication. It was
concerning the quick decisions which I
made right after the bridge shootings,
in fact, that I first applied the
counsel of her wisdom and presence.
First I called Stevie, pulling no
punches.

"Stevie this is Rick and I have
bad news." I said. She quietened.

"One minute ago, Jules was shot in
the head by a sniper, and I'm fairly
sure she's dead. So if you have any
input for me now, go ahead with it.
You're the first contact I've made. My
next communication will be with the
shot-caller."

"Rick, she doesn't have really any
family, not as such, but there are
friends everywhere. And as you know,
she's from Austin."

"We're in Baltimore. Austin's a

twenty-four-hour drive from here but it's closer than Phoenix." I said. "After I call headquarters, unless they sell me instructions otherwise, I'll drive her to the nearest fire station and provide the bare facts. So I would appreciate it if you would take a quick poll, find out if mail needs to go to Austin or Phoenix, and get back to me real soon."

forty-three.

Any unscheduled incoming call from Jules' number was enough to alert our operators of something awry. There was little need for many words, few were spoken, I gave the necessary biological and geographic details without using any names.

"Yeah what." came a voice over the line.

"It's bad news. We lost personnel while exiting the second detail, a bullet through the back glass, head shot. I'm en route to the nearest fire station. She'll go to Austin or Phoenix. By the time I drop her off, I should know which to tell them." I said.

"Good luck." The conversation ended. Stevie called back.

"It'll be Austin." she said. "Sending her back to Phoenix might blow her cover."

"Thanks. But I'll be back to Phoenix in a few days, if I can get out of here timely and orderly. You mind?"

"See ya when I see ya."

Minutes later, I pulled up to the front curb of a fire station, got out, and rang the front buzzer. In a half minute, an EMT/firefighter emerged to whom I gave bare facts.

"My partner was shot under I-95 at the East Bay during a narcotics cointel operation." I pointed at the car. "In there. I think she's dead." The medic followed me to the vehicle and searched for Jules' vitals. He looked at the back glass, then at me, and I nodded. "Maybe a bullseye on the pituitary."

From one of several cargo pant pockets the medic pulled a two-way radio and called for a stretcher. I heard the tone-out over the air dispatching for a possible nine-zero-one gunshot victim at the station. Additional medics came outside in the next half minute. One of them, the on-duty brass, tapped my shoulder and pulled me aside. I gave actionable, minimum logistical info.

"At first, there was some confusion whether she goes to Austin or Phoenix." I said. "Upon further review, Austin is her destination."

"I just heard from some people and now they want to hear from you." said the captain, handing me a wireless phone. The conversation was brief, the question was simple. What did I need to get out? In my mind, aside from potential local personality conflicts, the bullet-riddled back glass was the most glaring catch. The person at the other end of the line asked me to return the phone to the station chief.

I never saw my sedan again but I was given a similar vehicle. The extra firearms and contraband bait also stayed in Baltimore. The chief handed me a set of keys from the top drawer of a nearby desk and showed me through a back door to my new ride. I gave no further information about myself and/or

Denver Day

Jules, no one asked for any, and I was
back at the hotel collecting our few
belongings by ten p.m. I left the
room key and a nice cash tip on the
dresser, loaded our shit into the car,
and started west.

That was it. Do you expect me to
say, "It wasn't supposed to go down
like this?" Shouldn't I? The problem
with saying that is it's probably not
true. And what of saying, "This was
meant to be?" Mustn't it have been
fated since it's a historical fact now?
Yet, given the same scrutiny, either
assessment could be incorrect. Anyway,
fresh facts of reality were availing
themselves as I began a long, solitary
haul on I-95.

She must have, forensically,
realized something was wrong. At some
point, the exact circumstance had
become clear to her. It may not have
been until after she was already

unconscious, although it's likely that she had fairer warning than that. One can sense it coming, you know. It's usually not much lead time, but generally it's enough to reevaluate the local situation and execute an attempt at correctional navigation. So, she had probably either ignored the warning signs, elected not to say anything, failed to properly correct the matter, or was truly taken by surprise. Maybe the phenomenon was obscured by our involvement in the other killings of the nearby moment; a lesson of instant karma for a teacher of instant karma. Maybe the importance of knowing one's own stink was a key lesson learned.

She's more effective this way. I think she realized it was going down, and let it happen, thereby invoking a terminal advantage for herself, and incidentally for our partnership, and even for me individually. She bonded a connection that I could elect to sever

but I wouldn't. Human agency readily
comprehends the incumbency of universal
being, where petty death kills not the
soul. Achieving blindness to such
reality requires rigorous pedagogy in
bad faith. Change is a biological
constant eo ipso there is no actual
death for the likes of us.

forty-two.

I didn't want to return to Phoenix
and I didn't have to, but I had no
particular place else to go and my
stuff was still there. A change of
venue wasn't necessarily a perfect
magic bullet anyway, I thought, since I
wasn't a short-timer in this game
anymore. When commitments become
convictions, people's karmic awareness
grows and the realization weighs
heavier that every sell-side has a
back-side.

Self-delusion isn't part of a
genuine solution for anything usually,
so one should attempt to reconcile
personal experience with assessments of
a more universal nature. I felt lucky
to have the opportunity to reflect upon
the world and my situation, and such
realizations proceeded as I drove. I
began thinking of the earth as a
sarcophagus. Jules had gotten herself
killed, but I was the one buried alive.
When trapped inside of a fucking grave,
does it matter whether one is on the
sunny side, the north end, or at
whatever relative position? I propose
to you that it does not. Hell, she was
free, for which she'd get no negative
citation from me, but the situation
tilted my overall consideration of
things toward the more vividly
unforgiving.

I mulled over the wisdom of
driving back to Austin first. Under
the circumstances, I judged that what I

Denver Day

did with my time henceforth would be
more important than where I did it.
But with that kind of outlook, one's
relationship with geography becomes
almost harshly utilitarian
notwithstanding that a location's
philosophical practicality has much to
do with its aesthetic.

        "Well, Tex, what's your
preference?"

        Nighttime highways bring me peace
where no glaring foreign sun overheats
my brains. Also, it was nice to be
moving because transience, regardless
of direction, is inspiring for the
writer in me. Buffalo. Buffalo we
are. Coyotes. I rode along on my
metal horse, talking to the ghosts of
old Moses the Transcendental Cat and
Tex the Bane of Barristas while that
sonvabitch V.F.W. sun scorched some
other section of the back forty.

Hipster Bricks

"I hope it doesn't spoil your fun beyond the wall of sleep, but I think I should find someone to stand in for your actual mass per volume."

I didn't want to go to Texas, or back to Florida either. I'd go to Phoenix but it wouldn't be practical to stay long. I continued to bear her standard so, respectfully, I wasn't wanting to haunt the chapel. I knew my decision about where to go next would come soon. I'd work a little, save a little, gather my shit, and leave. Maybe the Rocky Mountains were the answer, I thought. How about Denver?

I set the dashboard radio to amplitude modulation and dialed in a proper all-night talk program, which always reminds me of the days, in-between college attempts, of my working as a graveyard-shift pizza driver. The topic of discussion for the hour was redheaded witches. Forty-eight hours

149

Denver Day

later, I made the Phoenix city limits,
by which time I was dead set on the
Mile High City.

I considered locking myself in my
apartment and sleeping for a week, but
after a day and a night of downtime
followed by a trip to the gym, I drove
over to Jules', Stevie's, and Queenie's
condo. Stevie knew it was me and had
the door open before I finished
knocking. She'd received a wire for a
sum of money from Jules' probated
estate, with instructions to distribute
it evenly among the roommates and me.
It was a large sum as far as I was
concerned, at twenty-five-thousand
dollars apiece.

"I'm moving to Denver."

"OK. We have people in Denver."

forty-one.

I prepared for new digs and gigs with a little help from our network. It could've taken me two moons to get turned around and back out of town, but it didn't. It took ten short days instead. Time was of the essence.

On the back side of Jules' transaction with the reaper was a pressing matter, an upswing stemming from our absolution of cocaine Bob and the two horse dealers. Namely, I had a surplus credit with the hegemons of sex and death. Stevie took notice of the extra credits, so she felt it was important that I do it in her butt while standing in the bathroom with Queenie watching. Jules wouldn't have had it any other way, in fact her commencement had upped my overall credit ratings on such accounts among various hegemons. Though not necessarily in the sense of deadline restrictions, there is a timeliness

factor for matters of sex and death,
respecting general temporal awareness
during key moments, in which failure to
take timely action is catastrophic.

Also, Queenie swallowed the whole
thing which I'd been careful not to
defile with soap since beginning my
relations with Jules. She was also
driven to drink the rest of my
decorations directly off Stevie's
lieutenant. Then, the two fair women
made sweet love to each other.

October lingered. Halloween
greeted me in Denver. I set out towing
the Ford I'd obtained in Baltimore
behind a rented moving truck. Snow met
me halfway, making a nail-biter out of
the Wolf Creek Pass. I could have gone
south of the mountains by way of New
Mexico's section of the Continental
Divide, but where's the logic in that
when there's a high mountain pass
alternative? The Rockies speak to me

152

from anywhere, but it's always nice to
actually see the family in person. The
flat lands are also talkative, I
wouldn't sell them short. Although
they lack the impressive reach
demonstrated by the mountains, the
lower lands of the desert southwest are
shallow seas of future and ancient
epochs with a strong local presence due
to the metaphysical attributes of
bodies of water.

I began settling into the Mile
High City and my new apartment.
Luckily, there was a diner-slash-
coffeeshop and a politically British
pub next door. My proximity to these
tables was no accident; I credited
Jules' very grace, Stevie's clerical
support, and general serendipity.
Jules' spirit kept me company with all
due presence, but a new driver was in
order. Of filling such positions
vacant, the ethical considerations were
imminent. Such reincarnations, when

properly contracted, denote the
beginnings of true greenfield
friendships which reach beyond the
scope of legacy heirdom because making
a new friend is always a reunion.

For the first few days, I stayed
in my apartment to write, read, think,
study, and acquaint with the new
personal quarters. It was blizzarding
anyway. On day four, first I went to
the pub, then over to the diner-slash-
coffeeshop. I don't drink but the pub
was large with a good kitchen and,
food-wise, a public house is what it is
regardless of who's poisoning whom with
ethyl alcohol in any given season. I
took a stool at a nook bar, and ordered
French fries, tomato soup, and iced
tea.

"Hey Rooster." Came a voice, from
a person two spots over. Sticking out
of a bulky coat and low hat was a head
and a mass of red hair. She moved to a

seat next to mine.

"Well hey yourself."

My food arrived. "Here you go, Ricky." The barkeep said, placing my meal before me. The fries were good, fresh cut, and the soup was perfect for the weather.

forty.

"Rooster, huh? But you're the red head."

"Yeah well I don't go around mirrors." Red said. She had on big clunky glasses, maybe she was farsighted too.

"Soup?"

"Oh yes." she said. "Perfect for the weather. How does the snow suit you?"

"Like socks on a cock."

The barkeep sat down across from us and sighed grandly, regarding me with what may have been a look of relief. Remembering something in the kitchen, he was off again.

"What are you working on?" I asked.

"Poetry. Some oil on canvas. Looking for a new roommate. If I may regard what you're working on, I think this place is in need of part-timers."

"Lucky." I said. "Today is the first time I've left my apartment."

"Are you an artist?" she asked.

"Sort of, yes. I'm a writer, mainly prose. I'm a student of history and philosophy, and not a scientist but I do have a recently renewed interest in mathematics. I have been traveling and had no good cause to stop, so I came here. I don't know how long I'll stay. A rolling stone gathers no moss but I'm taking a windbreak."

"Yes the muse requires forward motion. And travel." she said. "It's good work to find, I'm grateful to be creative talent."

The bar displayed Red's soup.

"Anyway, we can put you on some shifts here starting tomorrow mid-morning." he added. "Chelsea, your soup, love."

"Thank you." she said. "You'll like Denver. I hope you own plenty of plaid."

"The same to you. I appreciate

the hospitality."

"Mi casa es su casa."

After we finished the soup, we walked around the block, and off into the dharma. The past was a memory, the future was an idea, and I and Chelsea Red were more than the sum of our parts. Family's family and it's bigger than any individual agent. Importantly also, I and she and we in some newly formed political trinity had moved beyond the capricious grasp of the world's whimsy. Jules' careful treatment had raised me to this enlightened water, although I'd been forever in training for it. My soul was in a robust position. We happened upon a cinema and decided to take a treat of the science-fiction/western hybrid film genre.

"If one doesn't date one's friends, one loses them."

She agreed. After sitting through end credits, we went to the diner/coffeeshop by the Britons' pub where we stayed until four in the morning, drawing on napkins and playing cards and chatting up other nocturnals. Before the sun returned, we walked over to hers and slept side by side in full pajamas head-to-toe, without even holding hands. Believe that.

thirty-nine.

"What's my man's name?" I asked the next morning, as I left my friend occupied industriously at one of my typewriters and departed for the Briton.

"Doesn't matter, they're all expecting you. But Marion, Jack, is who brought us our soup yesterday. I'll catch up with you at eight."

Denver Day

The front door was the simplest
aspect of the Briton's footprint.
Somewhere in the middle of the house, I
found an office, where I asked of a
black-shirted dude whose name I didn't
catch, after Mr. Marion.

Working at a bar can be an eye
opening experience, even for jaded
fatalists. It's difficult to forget
how badly drunk is a major percentage
of the population in the United States,
but it never loses its shock value to
me. Many but not all bar patrons are
drunks, although alcohol by way of its
associations carries unethical baggage,
and its presence weakens risk pools and
ethical baselines remarkably.

In addition to my jaunt as the
pizza man during college, I worked in
various other restaurant service
positions that had incidentally
provided a handy background for my

shift work at the Briton. A nice
stream of people visited my nook bar
during the lunch rush, overall an
amicable crowd among which, during that
very lunch hour, I knew friendships
would be made and problems rooted out.
The muse was there but I didn't see
Jack Marion that day. My reliever
arrived at six o'clock.

I reconciled my till and bagged up
the black, counted my tips and went to
the office to square up with the books.
That afternoon I walked with two
hundred fifty dollars in cash.
Leaving, I stopped next door at the
diner where I befriended a waitress and
entered discussion about the merits of
skin ink. Plans were made for us to
shop together for new body art. After
a little while, I went home to shower
away the layer of restaurant film from
my skin insofar as that's not
impossible.

Denver Day

Surely two is better than one, if
you will, or three's better than two
but Jules' temperament was more of a
kind with the inked waitress' than
Red's. While I waited for Red to come
poking around, I kept thinking of what
exactly I had inherited from Jules.
I'd been apprenticed as a sidekick to
her enforcement of karmic law, and now
I was the principal of the operation.
Having a patron like Jules was changing
my moxie. Ethical oversight is an
obligation which, apparently, makes
things less safe. But even if that's
true, it should be philosophically
irrelevant, beyond possibly improving
one's definition of safety. By Jules'
example, truth in right action is
always safer than its absence. And
where did it get her? Enlightenment.
Transcendental existence. Lifetime
dedicated staff, and permanent free
room and board.

Red entered without knocking.

"You may take a day shift again
tomorrow, or you can close if you'd
rather." We returned to the diner
where I watched my peers from a
shifting vantage, as a squall of
justice percolated from a tiny,
undefined itch in my mind.

thirty-eight.

We counted cards and talked with
the diner's many nocturnal creatures.
At one in the morning, out of the blue
with style, grace, and all due respect,
Red asked me a question.

"Would you prefer a drop off or
pick up?"

"Drop." I said. Call me lazy
maybe, but it seemed like a no-brainer.

She changed the subject,
ostensibly. "How many cards do you

need?"

One aspect of Jules' philosopher's
stone related to preserving the
integrity of one's community and among
humanity in general: Regarding the
implements of keeping the peace in
one's world whether by public inquiry
or private investigation, maybe it's
helpful to think of it as police work.
If not, others may not either, and then
the door's wide open for more than just
political failure.

The simple truth is, justice is
more lucrative than injustice. The
buck must stop somewhere, long and
tall. That we could obtain the shit in
the first place in order to sell it,
meant that everyone upstream of the
particular matter at hand, for one
reason or another had passed the buck.
Then there came Jules. Then us. Now
me. In a bull market. The extent to
which my or our reputations preceded me

or us, or that specific news of our recent work had reached Chelsea Red and Jack Marion and company, seemed obvious to me based on their having rolled out the red carpet.

The foregoing perspective of justice as a community value seems to hold true at least for unpopular criminal activity and society's responses to it. Alternatively, popular criminal activity is a different story. For example, one reason why so-called white collar crime enjoys so many institutional loopholes is because of its relationship with the supply and demand of street crime. Criminal organizations understand this. The most effective lynch-pin for successful racketeering organizations is the occupation of public office. Nevertheless everything has a bottom, and while the intestines of beasts vary in length, what comes out of their ends is always shit.

The free markets respond with a natural luster to the strong supply and demand for cocaine. If the old money does not wish to deal with the logistics of dodgy street level operators then it can buy in bulk, directly from a wholesaler, e.g. through international trade agreements. This is an exception to assumptions that civil transgressions are always of less moral turpitude than statutorily codified felonies. It is a high crime when groups of people, even entire continents full of them or daresay planetsful, are subjugated in order for small rich communities to powder noses without getting hassled by, or syphilis from, the wrong kind of, or incorrectly jacketed denizen from a lower social class.

Also remember, just because an action is violent doesn't mean it's unjustified. Here I am not, for example, talking about capital punishment where a poor motherfucker sits in solitary confinement for twenty years before an old cuckold finally comes in to shove the prisoner full of cyanide and strychnine as an ancient monster in a collar stares on while jerking off. Historically, capital punishment was considered an act of expedient mercy, but twenty years in prison followed by a publicly fetishized, ritualized execution is something entirely else. When death's due it's to be served promptly otherwise it festers and damages the dharma, with bad karma ensuing.

"I have a tattoo shopping appointment with a new friend during the regular business hours so maybe I'll try out the night shift tomorrow." I said.

"Yeah, I heard. Her name's Sam Mary." said Red. "She's on the early shift in the morning. You can catch her when she gets off if you stop by here at noon."

thirty-seven.

We gave up on poker at the decaf diner at four a.m., and there'd be plenty of time for more of that in our bright and gaping future. This time, Red went to her house and I went to mine. When I got home I found a note from her, under the type bar of the machine she'd been using that morning, that read,

"People come and people go but friendship's forever. Show up and work whenever you like. Yours, Red. P.S., Are you getting a dagger or a lady with your torture tattoo? Or both."

Silly, I thought. That wasn't my card, no more than any other individual one. But for never say never, everyone needs a full deck and the fuller the better. I closed the curtains and worked at my desk until seven, then took a second night until eleven. I showered and went out to catch Sam Mary finishing the diner's first shift. She took off her waist apron when I showed up.

"What's up Sam."

"What's up Ricky. Shall we?" Breathing Denver air we hit the Denver pavement. A ten minute walk later we were in the body art establishment of her choosing.

"Are these guys sober?" I asked.

"Yep."

"Anything specific on your mind?"

"I have an appointment."

Denver Day

     She sat in one of the operating
chairs. Off came Sam's pants as the
staff made preparations. The doc began
to ink a twisting red candy stripe on
her right leg. A third of an inch
thick, it spiraled upward from behind
the knee to the butt cheek. Another
staffer, momentarily idle, offered me
some unscheduled chair time. I pulled
a notebook from the back pocket of my
jeans, thumbed to a particular sketch,
and handed it over.

     "Can do. Where do you want her?"

     I gestured, dropped my trousers,
and on the back of my left thigh she
began an octagonal trump. The
priestess of wands.

     "Who are you?" I asked Sam,
afterward.

     "Good question."

170

"Answer me."

"I am here, as are you. Anything more specific than that would be fiction, or pure conjecture bound to circumstantial restrictions. That's the best answer I have. The bonus answer is, now is now." she said. "You. Who, or what, are you?"

"A thoughtful answer with which I disagree, I say we aren't here and it's not now, our bodies are a contrivance, and this scene is a hustle although the odds are favorable. At least they favor us. How's your credit?"

"I am a cash-only operation."

I walked with her, to her apartment where we chilled in her book-filled den and burned incense for the rest of the afternoon. At five I went home and prepared for another shift at

the Briton, where I arrived at six-
thirty. The evening crowd came and
went. There were many food orders that
night, and the late crowd reliably
resumed its motion about town as the
dinner rush settled. Red visited at
eleven.

"Your drop is downtownish, not far
from here, actually. Go tonight if
you're ready."

"Fine. I'll get to it after I'm
finished here at two-thirty."

"I have a briefcase for you.
It'll be in the middle office, locked,
and here's the key. You can pick it up
when you cash out."

She pulled a stainless steel key
from her blouse pocket, gave further
instructions about the job and its
location, and sat at my bar until one.
I tidied up when the Briton closed at

two, cashed out, and retrieved the case
from the middle office as instructed.
Red's directions led me to the parking
lot of a shopping center ten minute's
drive from my apartment, so I walked
home to get my car first. While I was
there, I also picked up my single-
action forty-four magnum and holstered
it under my coat. Those small hours
were far colder than could've been
expected of any late October morning in
Phoenix certainly, although it's a fact
that nighttime weather in Phoenix is
typically pleasant.

The strip mall's commercial
tenants kept regular daytime business
hours so the parking lot was empty at
three in the morning. On the west end
of the lot, halfway between the street
and the store fronts, was a car fitting
the description of my contact vehicle.
I parked two spots away from it.

At my apartment, I'd checked the

briefcase's contents. It contained
three kilo bricks of cola. I sat for a
minute in my vehicle, letting some
calmness permeate me and my scenery
before proceeding. As I walked up, a
person waved at me from the driver seat
of the contact vehicle. Down the
window rolled and I handed over the
briefcase. The individual set it on
the passenger seat without opening it.
There were no words. I drew the forty-
four and shot the stranger in the
middle of the skull, from the back of
which brains splattered the passenger
seat.

thirty-six.

    I'd not been briefed regarding the
identities or affiliations of the
person who I just killed. Typically I
wouldn't be and I did ponder briefly at
mud's web of life up to the final cut.
Someone had an actionable opinion about

the late buyer or else I wouldn't have
been there, and that level of certainty
had to be good enough for me under the
circumstances. I knew the Denver
Police Department could make better
sense of the situation if they came
upon the briefcase filled with mister
white, which I left on the seat,
covered in brains.

Meanwhile, if this was not what
Red and Jack Marion had in mind, then I
don't know what to tell you. Of course
it had to be, and as far as I was
concerned, it was. In addition to my
passing regard for the deceased buyer,
I was curious after my unknown
colleagues on the sell side of the job,
like an ad hoc jury of my own peers, as
it were. That's civics. It's how
civil action works. Which means that
public agency involves the girl next
door, and grandma, and the little
league coach, and farmer brown's wife
as much as it was or is you and me and

Denver Day

the mayor or anyone else. It's self
government. American democracy.

    I realized that I was out of order
in not having Sam with me, though.
Arguably. Working alone could be good
for a higher profile assassination, but
not necessarily for common street
sweeping. Well, it's all street
sweeping really, but part of my point
is that not having a quorum at hand can
even be thought of as a disservice to
the citizen getting the bullet. I'm
still new at this, I thought.
Knowledge grows with experience.

    That night's job was a new and
different sort of transaction for me.
Not so procedurally, but aesthetically
and karmically. And not that it was
bad karma, but it was different karma
than if Jules had been with me, or even
Sam. I knew there was probably some
good reason for my omitting Sam on the
detail, because I make steady conscious

176

and subconscious efforts at preventing undesirable philosophical accidents. But since I'd begun carrying surplus credit with the hegemons of sex and death, chances were that it wasn't any discrepancy on those accounts. One remarkable difference between bringing and not bringing Sam along that night could've been that it wasn't necessary. It may have been redundant, for example, or her company might have resulted in the occlusion of some key personal learning experience for me.

I decided not to go knocking at Red's or Sam's door in the hour following my service of death's process, and went to the diner instead, for the warmth and regularity of the night crowd's card playing, chess, drawing, writing, eating, and drinking espresso. I was grateful to bump into Sam, of course.

"I didn't want to bug you while

Denver Day

you were trying to close, so I waited
here." she said. "How was your first
night shift?"

"Well it wasn't my first night
shift ever, but it was fine thank you.
Although there is high ambient exposure
to barroom trivia and I'm unsure if
that's a good thing."

An old-fashioned analog snow was
coming down outside. Through the
double-paned windows we watched falling
flakes, large as muffins.

"And your new candy stripe?"

"Feels bloody good. Speaking of
cards, let's." She winked and shuffled
out a tarot set. Red used standard
Bicycles but Sam was an historical
purist. "Such talents fade without
use."

"I've always wanted to draw a deck

of my own, however the writer's muse can be selfish." I said. "Although I make no formal complaint on that measure, and it's no excuse for lack of diversity in one's creative output."

"Maybe you should make a set of runes. That wouldn't take as long."

As we conversed, my awareness of time's passing heightened. Time of a certain kind. How long would I be in Denver before the wanderlust struck again? Such preoccupations come with the territory, I thought. Since a diversity in setting is important to the living muse, domestic impermanence is an occupational hazard for writers.

For example, I may define the amount of time worth spending in any given area as, the minimum period it takes me to develop an authoritative prosaic perspective of it. Some locations give more than others, of

course. I'm learning not to
overspecialize, keeping in mind that
location is a variable factor. The
time it takes for a given writer to
make a place varies. For example, one
could probably spend a lifetime in
Baltimore without exhausting the full
exploration of its myriad nooks,
crannies, and jewels but that city gave
me a life's work in a few hours.

     "I usually walk but tonight I
drove." I said.

     "Yeah I heard. You ready?"

thirty-five.

     As I've related up to now, our
self appointment as karma police
evolved into efforts at intercession
and right action among the narcotics
black market. Then Jules was killed
and I took up her mantle, among other

old habits.

However.

The hatcheting of dealer-managers might send a strong message to administrators, but a greater complexity was looming larger over me after my first detail in Denver.

Access to capital gives political protection to marketplace operators. For example, if they lose an agent, a new person can be put into the breach to resume the dirty work. This is an injustice that's occluded amid complicated scenarios. A complication of bureaucracies, but not individuals working alone as in Jules' barista incident.

I was thinking maybe I could circumvent such an inefficacy in our methodology, by taking a harder look up a command chain. In doing so, I could expect to be on my own, research-wise and logistically. But there would be tacit support from my current associates and from the transcendent and sublimely watchful Jules. I really wished she were there to consult in the flesh, nevertheless, good faith is one of the keys for transmigration of the soul.

Apathy is an excellent painkiller. Usury and other such crimes in the offing don't drive anyone crazy if nobody gives a shit. I can pay a tax and remain objective, assuming taxes assessed in good faith are the appropriate way to pass the buck. With such a perspective among the greater marketplace of ideas, beyond the trappings of petty theft, doors begin to open for truth and adventure of a higher order. It's a bull market where opportunity knocks when one's brain is not clouded by rat poison and money.

Despite my argument that leadership presents more economical targets, I still entertain the notion that different fruits of the same poison tree are easily interchangeable. But, with all due caveats of fact checking, the corporate media and popular electoral politics may serve no better purpose than to finger outstanding greaseballs overdue for fine tuning.

Prior to statehood, the only people brave enough to self-identify as agents of the early Arizona territorial government seem to have been train robbers, and it somehow led to today's Arizona prostitutes who wear actual price tags on themselves. Imagine my dismay, as a square, when I discovered that. Such is the nature of running a railroad. Alternatively, the earliest administrators of the state of Colorado were squatting mountaineers, who perhaps set a precedent for

contemporary Denver's apparently more
sensible prostitutes. Or maybe, in
large measure, I am totally incorrect
in these assessments because key
information has been lost in the
translation or transmission. I'm just
telling you what I think I saw.
Anyway, for various reasons, I had a
notion that if someone were to choose a
city in which to start a business for
the purpose of greasing shitball
politicians, Denver could be a tenable
market.

Incidentally, in Denver the sex
workers were in place, or, well, the
ones supporting the business class
were, but they were more subtle than
the ones in Phoenix, in my view. In
Phoenix, the freelancers at least,
seemed to have done a terrible job, as
a class, at researching their client
demographic. Or maybe not and I was
just in the wrong place. I have
trouble with price tags on anything,

because economics is such a politically
charged issue for me.

Meanwhile, in the predawn hours of
our infinite youthful adulthood, Sam
and I drove home from the diner. I
looped by the shopping center lot where
I'd eliminated someone's underling
earlier that morning, and thought again
of how the message might be interpreted
by the target organization, if it was
understood by anyone.

"Do you have any political
aspirations." I asked.

"That depends. Theoretically yes.
But practically speaking, I'd be asking
how a given campaign is worth the
trouble in a technical sense." she
said. "Because remember, a certain
kind of peace can be found in the cold
logic of apoliticality, be it right or
wrong. Nevertheless, politics is
important and family is forever, and

vice versa, therefore you and I are like an old married couple in real ways. In the most positive sense, of course. We're all professionals here, and it happens that our political disposition is partially owing to your reputation's preceding you. You're in full comeuppance and I'm here for you just as you are for me. That's how it's been throughout the history of the universe. Park over here on the street under that tree and come on upstairs with me. We'll take a nap. I'm on afternoon shift today."

"Me too, I suppose."

I parked and we went up. Unlike Jules, Stevie, and Queenie, she lived alone, like Red.

"Are today's tattoos enough to accommodate quid pro quo activity for us right now?" she asked.

It was a question worth examining. Tattoos do involve blood.

"Probably." I said. "Even if it weren't, I should have sufficient credit to cover any odd fart."

thirty-four.

It is one thing to fix assholes in dark parking lots and under bridges. That's simple, more or less. But identifying some public figure or official worth fixing presents a more nuanced (if potentially more entertaining) operation. Underneath a bridge, the asshole is easy to find and less prevaricating. But in a political arena or public eye occurs far less straight-shooting than in sewers, and these realms' overlapping doesn't improve their standards. Nevertheless, inexact fuzzy data are how come tea leaves are readable.

"Politics." Sam echoed me. "Why?
Are you going international?"

"It could come to that, keep it in
mind. Although, because all politics
are local, I should probably start at
home."

"Nobody ever said we couldn't be
polyvocational." she said.

"I don't want to spoil any
existing relationships." I said.
"Anyway, I suppose the local news is as
good a place as any to start.
Otherwise, I'm open to any inside info
you can dig up."

"Actionable intelligence is
actionable intelligence, work's work,
and I don't mind helping you under one
condition."

"What?"

"Sexual favors." she said. "Right now."

"I do feel like I've earned it today. Do I remind you of anyone?" I said.

"Yeah you do. Otherwise I wouldn't have signed on for this gig." she said.

We spent the rest of the morning on her giant couch. Later at the Briton, commencing my afternoon shift, I actually turned on and paid attention to the television, which is a rare occurrence. I am so sorry but I did, because I was wondering what the hegemons of the slobbering mass media dog, in all of its worm-covered glory, might deliver to me.

Some guy came in and sat at the bar. "What are you watching?" he

Denver Day

asked.

"Good question. I'm trying to
figure out who should get the axe. So
to speak."

The topic interested him, judging
by the look on his face. He ordered
soup. I watched the screen with a
newfound interest. The program was a
daytime talk show out of Los Angeles,
featuring guests chatting around a
table on the subject of climate change.
The panel included an I.T.
entrepreneur, a U.C.L.A. professor
emeritus, and a representative from a
non-governmental organization.

thirty-three.

Viewing that conversation about
climate change among the electric glory
hole intelligentsia, sent me down my
old faithfully well-traveled path of

questioning why there are so many
people on this third rock from the sun,
and why I'm not the only one here.
Professor McKenna put it simply that
"rocks people," as apple trees apple.
In all its brevity, the statement is
true enough. But before I slip into
some perfunctory apology for having
solipsistic fantasies, it's worth
pointing out that, in light of the
insect- and plant-like (and rock-like)
nature of the hybrid that's the human
diaspora, such philosophical questions
aren't fanciful.

There are civil ways to resolve
large scale people problems like
planetary overcrowding. I'm not
speaking of genocide, whether or not by
its common and popular modes of the
weak nuclear force or poisonous gas.
There are subtler and pleasanter ways
to apply metaphysics. I'm not saying
that I do or don't have all the
answers, but I am saying that right

Denver Day

answers can exist. The perspective of
an endlessly optimistic engineer is the
only tractable collective attitude for
a society who wishes to thrive,
persevere, and solve complex problems.
And it's never too late to mend.

As a consolation prize for not
clearing the cull, the accommodating of
egomaniacs to bear heraldry and titles
which license their lordship over crime
and filth, isn't part of any real,
thoughtful solution. Neither is any
meat market for intergalactic whore
mongers. Where there's a flesh market,
there's cocaine and that's where I may
forego the weak force and advocate
application of the strong nuclear
force, you know, gravity. Local
Newton. Bosons. High velocity. An
object in motion has a tendency to stay
in motion unless acted upon by an
outside force. Anyway, cocaine seems
to have such an effect on people. When
regularly under the influence, it seems

too good not to kill for.

Planet Earth Sol Charlie is getting too crowded with humans (again) and the very intergalactic nature of the human genome is a key aspect of the challenge. At such a small-scale local level, one hand doesn't know what the other's doing. Local cohesion is needed for handling problems like overcrowding and resource conservation on any given terrestrial platform. Demography, for example, is important in this matter for the purpose of determining who's who, and where, for a functional ward system that protects the progeny regardless of the faults of its ancestors.

Someone should invent hats, and then everyone could simply stack the generations on top of one another per aspera ad astra. My keenness on this issue has developed partly as a result of my working "undercover" or

Denver Day

"embedded" for too long as an
investigative reporter, which has led
me to conduct too much people-watching.

As horrible as it is, racial or
gender coercion or discrimination in
bad faith, is fairly obvious to behold,
forensically. But the thickness of
general improvidence can be even more
snowblinding. "Creeping malaise"
usually and appropriately is a phrase
turned in a context of economic dialog,
as economics is, in fact, applied
social politics. It's a nice way to
say the world's mostly full of
ignoramuses who deserve to die as
quickly as possible before they waste
any more air. But as an ethicist, the
stupidity of others can become one's
own problem, easily. Unfortunately.

Responsible action regarding
people · (or political) problems on our
(or my) rock obligates us (or me) to
conduct a witch hunt for which it can

be said, there are two main rights of
way: the front door and the back door.
For me to elaborate on this point
sufficiently could take forever, so for
now I'll just remark that everyone has
a set of applicable skills and I
request that you please use them for
the sake of us all. Moving forward, as
events occur, I will try hard to give
color analysis and credit where it's
due, about skills and techniques for
life's doors.

    "Pretty good fookin' soup." said
the guy at the bar.

    "It's on the house."

thirty-two.

    The front door involves the world
of first sight. Qualia. You know,
ontological stuff. Appearances,
labels, words, colors. Outward nature.

Denver Day

The butler with the broomstick in the
bedroom, and long division. But the
back door (these are my terms, and
they must mean something different at
some other ladies' bridge club), ain't
linear. The back way is an animal
hunt, and it may involve cute furry
kittens but that's typically not what
people hire me for. The tools of back
door investigations include instinct.
Back is the path by which, using the
sense of smell, one differentiates
between two business executives who are
identical, except that one's crooked
and the other isn't. It's not
necessarily harder than front-of-the-
house work, just different.

   The back door is how one finds
unadvertised or unknown loopholes.
It's witch hunting not in the sense of
targeting bloodsucking nature, but by
the more general interdiction of
derelictions that manifest among the
living. People aren't patently evil,

but may have a definite hand in
becoming that way. Over time, they can
become evil although then they aren't
really people anymore, rather only part
of a nature that's set for a cull.
Such essence is dispatched as a point
of order.

The promising child they once were
can be revisited, but whatever darkened
future lines happen to be involved are
finished. The tree-like nature of
connections among space, time, and
living allows for this remedy. The job
is to seal the terminal end of a path
into nowhere and darkness, and pipe the
original individual spirit back to some
historical restore point. Regardless
of specific procedure, flushing out
sleepy evil from daily life requires a
certain illumination.

The reason I bring all of this up,
is that hunting for dirty politicians
involves investigative nuances

popularly thought to be occult.
Interlopers aren't well received by
politically deft creatures because of
the real threats which strangers and
the unknown pose to the efficacy of
conspiracy. Hence no timely front-door
inquiry can be relied upon entirely,
because operators as bureaucrats in
advantageous positions of leverage, are
sheltered within a partisan cottage
industry. But they're predictable.
Real live politicians must move around
to go to the toilet, or to dinner.

When it's swimming nearby, one can
feel its draft. Leviathan is
squeezable but it's not easy and makes
Jaws look like a pussy. Angling
efforts often leave its pursuers
holding no more than a handful of fur
and feathers; like a wrecked
politician in the quail bag, for
example, while the actual source
persists. It must be a part of human
nature, that we combat such agency for

our own sake. Recognizing humanity's
weaknesses is a key to reconciliation
thereof. Because the work requires
some minimum distance, it can be done
from nearly anywhere or when, hence the
gamelike nature of the task is obvious.

Red visited me at the Briton at
two that afternoon, the first time I'd
seen her since the parking lot detail.
Still trawling around for winners, I
switched the t.v. over to C-SPAN,
and she gave me a quizzical glance.

"Just canvasing the public sphere
for personnel issues." I said. "Civic
duty, you know."

"You are quite the public
advocate, Rick." she said.

"How's your side of the high life,
Red?"

"Pretty quiet. Are we on for

cards at the diner tonight?"

"Yeah buddy. If you don't mind, stop by my apartment first. Could you hand me that newspaper, please?"

Profiteering is a kind of racketeering, avarice is a chain to hell, but a true quid pro quo economy can be most egalitarian. I was increasingly determined to find the right someone screwing around on the public coin in bad faith so I could sew them up in a snare of their own making. Then, maybe we could take our show out on the high seas. The third shift arrived at seven and I walked, carrying my newspaper, with a tip total as robust as the first day's.

thirty-one.

A half hour after I got home, Red arrived.

"So what's on your mind?" she asked. I beckoned her over to my kitchen table.

"Frankly, there is much work to be done." I suggested, showing her a photo in the newspaper. "But for this detail, maybe Sam's too green to come along by herself."

"I'm listening." she said, looking at the photo. "Who are these assholes?"

"They're candidates for state and federal office, all campaigning for the election next month. They're meeting downtown tonight at the Sheraton for a swanky partisan fundraising dinner." I said, pointing at one of the faces. "This particular guy is director of a corporation with a multi-billion-dollar market share of global coffee, and incidentally, therefore, international cocaine too. He also has oil and gas assets in the Piceance Basin and he happens to be running for governor. The man isn't predicted to win the popular vote but there are many uses for political campaigning, beyond popularity.

"How do you feel about the direct influence of the South American cocaine crop's futures market upon policy in colorful Colorado?" she asked.

"For what it's worth, I'm against it in every way. His incumbency is hereby remanded to yesterday's committee." I said. "And we're working late tonight. If we're staking out that hotel, we should leave right now."

"Let's go by the pub and stock up on sandwiches." Red said. "And then to the diner for Sam."

I had gotten into the action with Sam and Red, in part, as an effort to invoke Jules, or honor her, or sate her hungry wandering spirit, or grow onward, or something. For the moment, I was still in violation of one of my governing ethical modes, but the matter was easily corrected; If I expected to retain my incumbency for Jules' favorable preternatural wardship, and to reconcile equanimity among the marketplace of the universe, then I needed to update my vesting guaranty with the hegemons of sex and death. Even dead people don't work for free.

We gathered our coats (and I gathered a rifle), loaded ourselves into my car, stopped at the pub for provisions, then picked up Sam from the diner. It was eight-thirty when we pulled into the hotel parking lot, and the fundraising wing-ding inside was already begun. In a more perfect world, we would've been there in time

·to see our man enter the building. Red
said she knew the kitchen staff and
went inside to do reconnaissance.

She returned with actionable
information a half hour later. "They
all came in by that big main front
door, and they'll leave by it
afterward, at ten o'clock. None of
them have rooms booked here, at least
not under their real names."

I appreciated that. I wouldn't
even have to get out of the car. The
three of us sat there for ninety
minutes, eating peanut butter and jelly
sandwiches on jalapeño sourdough bread,
drinking San Pellegrinos, and watching
the hotel's front door. The parking
lot was reasonably lit, though it was
nookish and shadowy and the weather was
gray and wintry. We were fifty yards
from the front main entrance and
situated to allow ourselves a clean
getaway from the lot without u-turns or

other potentially calamitous bullshit.
Next to me in the seat, the barrel of
my loaded thirty-aught-six poked down
into the floorboard. Patiently we
waited, watching.

Eventually, Red called it coming
down: "Here comes the party." And so
it did. A group was trickling out at a
lazy after-dinner pace.

"There." she said. "Right there
he is, putting on a red scarf."

Quietly and quickly I put that
barrel out the window and braced it
against the side mirror, and set the
cross-hairs on the head of the
strolling cocapolitico.

thirty.

I squeezed gently. The oily
coffee trader hit the pavement like

205

water dumped from a five gallon bucket.
I slid the rifle back into the
floorboard and put the car into gear.
The shot turned heads but triaging the
casualty took precedence and no one
properly spotted us, evidently. As we
drove away, a crowd was gathering
around the fallen man. We entered
traffic and merged back onto the
thoroughfare.

"Well, doobie-doobie-doo." I
said, after several moments of silence
from my passengers.

"Take the car home and we'll walk
to the diner." Red said.

"Who was that?" asked Sam.

Instead of making a beeline for
the diner, the three of us went inside
my apartment to cover our action with
the relevant hegemons. Nobody was
coming after us for that job,

nevertheless the time was now for
housekeeping and the diner could wait
another twenty minutes for rocks off.
At that, I and Red gave special
attention to Sam's holiest of holies.
In fact, we even added a little green
tea. There is no cause to get all
mushy and long winded after a good
sniping. Maybe during a camping trip
it's fine to drag out the process for a
lunar cycle or two. But there's never
good cause for a full-length production
when veggie smoothies and a nice game
of gin await.

It was snowing a few flakes. En
route by foot to the diner for cards,
drawing, and discussion of truth and
beauty among friends and strangers, the
time was eleven-forty-five. We sat.
Sirens, passing by, were heard every so
often. At two in the morning, Sam's
arcane deck replaced Red's moderns and
we made use of its holistic
assessments.

A key aspect of scrying anything is to be mindful that things are what they are, not what they aren't. Auspicious and optimistic card spreads that morning tracked our party of three's continuing along current trajectories of truth and justice happily while avoiding harmful trappings of the profane world. For us and the likes of us, the general indication was of useful and successful sailing, even if it wouldn't always be perfectly smooth. Another useful thing to remember about many arcane decks is, because the card faces often are so "busy," one may leave the same spread tabled for a long while, allowing new associations to continue surfacing.

The hour of six o'clock beset us and our fellow patrons. On our way out, I picked up a freshly delivered edition of the *Post*. We went to Sam's and slumbered.

twenty-nine.

An unmarried write-in candidate
runs for precinct committee, and
accusations of spousal abuse are a real
possibility before the election
arrives. But whack a handful of
narcotics traffickers and a politically
active neocapitalist, and even the
fucking mailman forgets your name.

That autumn in the Mile High City,
it was obvious the hegemons of sex and
death weren't the only ones active
among the cosmogony. The tedious fact
that many are in the service of the
wrong demigods was also increasingly
apparent. Such widely misappropriated
allegiance and support-in-kind can
generate undesirable prevailing winds.

Many people are so intoxicated and
confused that they don't realize the

dystopian world around them can be
fixed. Granted, this little world is
cosmologically rural and the nature of
backwater colonies is what it is; and,
the issue of class is unavoidable,
daresay even in the United States where
liberally applied benefit of the doubt
can grant quarter to ne'er-do-wells.
With sufficient political support,
sure, one may go comfortably and
unmolested for a night on earth. But
if not, then your miserable forgotten
death in a slag heap mud pit probably
pleases whoever happens to live
upstairs from you, as long as they also
get their pound of flesh. Such are
houses and so goes civility in the
context of striving and desperation,
regardless of the specifics of any
ideology or governing writ.

    But anyway, the man who died in
front of the hotel, well, his politics
and business among the economic and
cultural strata are commonplace against

the backdrop of a terrestrial
backwater. His own people didn't seem
to give a shit, and his death even
compared with Jules' in its general
lack of impact upon the subject's
continuation of daily business and
keeping up appearances. Death can be a
good career move. Both the agent and
the entourage may continue operating,
with enhanced second sight. This is
why the trajectory of the living truly
matters.

   Anyway, it is taught that removal
of such politicos like so many rotten
teeth is a high crime. But crimes
against entire galaxies of people,
resource rape, caste lodging and
subjugation, and systematic plowing-
under of populations who are fully
intellectually capable of governing
themselves properly, that's supposed to
be alright? I say, it's worth the
effort to find out exactly who is
teaching such a contradictory,

unamerican lesson and at the end of
that research rainbow I guarantee true
criminals are to be found. Point out
that taxation without representation is
illegal and an attorney will respond
immediately from the District of
Columbia two thousand miles away to say
otherwise regardless of the litigant's
legitimacy or the facts of the case.
Shoot a politician good or bad and
nobody cares, but threaten a
bureaucrat's usury-based salary in hell
and you'll be bent to will under a gun.

Autumn turned to winter and we
never heard anything personal regarding
the gubernatorial candidate's demise.
The elections came and went. The snow
was nice. I watched the flakes fall
during my afternoon shifts at the pub,
and at night through the big front
windows of the diner.

I reflected upon the various
hegemons represented in the faces of

Sam's tarots. Avarice. Vice.
Gluttony. License. Beauty. Peace.
Love. Knowledge. War. Hate.
Confusion. Death. Fate. Doom.

    The events in Baltimore grew ever
more distant in my rearview mirror.
Jules was relatively quiet that winter
from beyond the grave. I mean, she was
still present, but there'd been
sufficient time for her personality to
integrate organically with Sam's and
Red's. The situation gave an
interesting reductionist perspective of
the human spirit, reinforcing the
understanding that we are all one, in
the broader context, over time. The
D.N.A. code says the same thing in a
different way. Historically, Jules the
woman was still with me, or us, and she
was as institutionally willing and
capable of helping as ever. By most
people she channeled easily.

    Our general operations were

underwritten by her spiritual equity
and in conformance with her political
will. In my world, Jules was at peace
insofar as it was possible for her to
be, which can be thought of as one of
several accurate ways to define death,
among so many of its poorer
definitions. For posterity, lives are
on the record, and the living are put
upon with the temporary task of
carrying on the infinite conversation,
by which those who are at peace can be
poured like so much ambrosia.

twenty-eight.

    At some point, if proceeding
correctly, a philosophical higher
ground prevails that's tantamount to
ego death. At such an end, I was
experiencing the unexpected thrill of
feeling dead and alive concurrently,
because 1) death had proven to be a
transcendental experience, in my view,

and 2) I'd walked into a career that
involved killing whereby within just a
few weeks, I went from unwitting
accomplice in a random assault on a
barista to an over-the-edge pro bono
vice cop.

    I was amazed that the day-to-day
implications of my very serious new
career, which was blossoming after
years of suffocating existentialism and
ethical preponderance, were so
surprisingly placid and bracing. Yes,
among the infinite flux, this freshly
undiscovered country was simply another
sea change in the due course of
infinite change, but the increasing
ubiquity of such moments was my zen.
Living a life of actual heroic first-
person live action drama while wearing
the shoes of the heroes of truth, love,
and justice doesn't seem to impress
people. But that should be read as an
indictment of society, not against
truth and love.

Denver Day

    Encountering such a comeuppance,
one realizes the privileged work of
greasing shitballs occasionally in good
faith could go on forever. But that
potential perpetuity or timelessness
begs philosophical questions of the
efficacy of the effort. In other
words, could I really go on forever
weeding out bad apples, yet never
witness any correlated improvement of
civilization? Talk to some retired
first responders or maybe some ex-
monastics about it because those groups
bear a certain level of hard-earned
nihilism.

    The quandary of "running to stand
still" delineates fate and free will,
therefore it gives some description of
fundamental aesthetic or metaphysics.
Quantum theory and Brownian motion
notwithstanding, digital physics and
cellular automata are facts of life.
When a totality of life's circumstances

are considered over a long period,
breakthrough deductions can be made.
For example, it's clear to me now that
life is a game. Or maybe it's better
to say that it always can be, often is,
and rarely isn't so why not.

I don't intend cynicism. Change
can be directed, people can be made
comfortable, darkness can be dispelled
and should be. The point is, universal
change is subtle if not slow, so under
the circumstances it follows there's
always more work to be done despite the
continuation of nonsense. Local
benefit can be achieved as a result of
one's efforts, though local
implementations can be dramatic enough
to distort any firsthand account.
These circumstances brought about a
certain elective aspect to my new work
content. Again, the world is very
gamelike, which belies its fundamental
construction and nature.

Denver Day

Such a confluence of earned
wisdom, while it is enlightening enough
to cause deep change and movement, is
not a surprising turn of events.
Change is said to be the only constant,
after all. An important reason such
judgment is so becoming is, these
realizations are intuitive and cogent
answers, to questions long studied by
all thinkers. Findings like these are
the whole point of such searching, and
they are part of why a lifelong quest
for truth and knowledge is worthwhile.

What to do now? How to avoid the
onset of complacency? What of the
ethical questions of killing people who
need to die in the local sense, but the
job is arbitrary, capricious, or
irrelevant in a more universal context?
Such variant contingency requires an
intermediary. Dear Jules. That's
approximately the narrow line we were
walking, to operate without imperiling
ourselves with the hegemons of

218

relevance.

"We could leave the states, yeah?"
Red said.

"Without the home field advantage,
would we be able to function with the
necessary impunity?" I wondered.

"Maybe. It depends on where we
go." Sam said. "But a rolling stone
gathers no moss."

"A move gives me more places to
call home, and more places about which
to write plausible nonsense regarding
what I am and where I've been." I
said. "Just as painters need a change
of scenery, eh Red?"

Sam, as a poet and esotericist,
gave no straight answer about her muse
pursuant to local geography or
cartography. "But I tell you one
thing. We're not fucking going to

Mexico." she said.

"Well, never say never, maybe we are." I said. "You're the reader of tea leaves, if the teasan says go to Ciudad Juárez, then, you know, we're going to Juárez."

"Mexico's too close, I think." she said.

"Well this is a democracy so with the C.I.A. as our travel adviser we'll go where we're welcome." I said.

twenty-seven.

The solstice came. Allover me. By the New Year, Red and Sam and I were jointly lodged and sharing household duties. The dynamic in our home reminded me of the focused bustle of Jules', Stevie's, and Queenie's place back in Phoenix. Sam was an evergreen

of warm vibrations, everything in her
draft and field was brilliantly alive
and thriving. She maintained a large
reef aquarium, nineteen ferns, and wise
wild-eyed vegan cats, as big as baby
bears with bushy colorful coats, who
requested in plain English to be fed
daily thrice. She was alive, an
excellent specimen of life. Nor were
Red and I any slouches around the
garden but living with a gem like Sam
was a windfall. She also wrote
constantly, either scribbling or typing
away, and she painted with oil to
confound any writer's burnout.

    I kept a pulse on the weather,
meanwhile keeping up with my writing
and studies. All three of us were at
peace, healthy, and in flux, thriving,
alive. One can always revisit such
times in the heart past, but the
straightaways of life are just another
part of a neverending journey. Paths
easily traveled allow for making good

Denver Day

time. Make hay while the sun shines.

    We worked our respective shifts at
the diner or the pub, spending much of
our time counseling drunks and bankers,
praying for bums, and playing gin. I
felt half-retired, frankly. After the
hotel job, there wasn't more "work"
for the remainder of that year. Mid-
January, Red came up with a heroin deal
that Sam took the lead on, and the gig
went off just fine. She basically
burned down some dude from the Midwest
with a sawed-off shotgun in the back
office of a filling station near the
airport. We left a duffel bag full of
product sitting on the dead man's
chest, who by rights had ventured too
far from his tri-state area. The
duffel bag probably ended up in a
proper evidence locker somewhere.
Again we received no material argument
from the proletariat ensuing the
matter.

Regarding our inclination or willingness to go international with our highly pastoral and aesthetic American shit show, we waited in the wings for some embassy to pick us up on waivers. Such is maritime law, we weren't complaining, and the speeds of slow boats vary. There is truly no time and we had plenty of it.

Eventually, I think Red got bored, and off she went to the police academy in Fort Collins. She wouldn't be gone long, only six weeks. Meantime, we'd be taking all, if any, necessary side work from Jack Marion at the Briton. The muse tugged at me but I argued back, that the quiet of the season warranted momentary stillness to better hear inspiration. The great American novel can be elusive and skittish in the bush and I was looking for a flock of them, so patience was due.

However, patience and quiet was

just as likely to render nets full of nothing but shitball politicos and other high-dollar bilge. That's alright though, because there's room for everybody in my back pages. One of many open secrets about writing novels is that writing them is more important than reading them. Nobody is supposed to give a shit if anyone reads it (and most won't). Especially not the author. An author works at the pleasure of his friends, anyway, not statistical strangers. Statisticizing people can be dangerous even if it's not done in bad faith. The more the merrier but for writers the number one is how success is measured in terms of readership. Two is great but it's a surplus.

Anyway, as Red farmed herself out to serve and protect, Sam and I closed the gap. The weather remained cold enough to hibernate and skiing was still an option for burning off the cash surplus we recognized as honest bartenders and waiters. With a little luck along the way, we'd find some coke dealers to shutdown. You people who are still doing blow really ought to stop, particularly those of you who know better. And if you don't know any better, think of this advice as process service: Quit while you're ahead.

Sam and I loaded up the car and made for Crested Butte, where we arrived one hour ahead of a three-day blizzard. We lodged at a reasonable chateau and began acquainting ourselves with locals and tourists while fresh powder accumulated without.

twenty-six.

We and our comrades at the lodge were giddy to get up the lift, as the little resort village dug out of the spring storm. We'd spent the past two

Denver Day

days chumming it up with an
entertaining and valuable assortment of
personalities around the lodge, playing
cards, sketching, scribbling, and
pulling all-nighters to yak with
strangers about drama and the profane.
But the baby sunshine was beautiful and
the powder was lovely and all of the
camp were through being cooped up
inside.

When visiting a new city, or maybe
rehashing my current backdrop, I always
ask myself, "where's the mayor?" It's
a fair question for weather-related
conversation and has fewer possible
answers than one might think.
Responses can include "the mayor is
right here," and "funny you should
ask, I'm the mayor, hello," and "I
don't know," or "there isn't one,"
or "it doesn't matter." Anyway, the
lodge's owners weren't there. The
management was limited to some
revolving plurality of lifers and part-

timers working the bar, where some
semblance of leadership should exist,
if only of purely symbolic eminence.

Communal lodging in Crested Butte,
Colorado, was reasonably peaceable.
The wet bar of the main lodge, where we
weathered much of the blizzard, was
running at any hour. For the moment, I
and Sam wore the only hat of narcotics
interdiction apparently, and among the
common spaces there was only one dealer
of any note. The game was teeners and
eight balls, small transactions.
People were snowed in, after all, and
vacationers wishing to drink straight
through the bad weather needed
something to stand them up.

Despite what our nature, over or
under, might have seemed to third
parties in the context of the
egalitarian marketplace of a jewel
among the Rockies, we had no immediate
cause for fixing that dealer's wagon

with extreme prejudice. Not yet. Not
technically. Dull as our ethical axe
was. But our vacation was still young
and sure enough, after the weather
cleared, some college kids arrived and
changed our laissez-faire perspective.
They were binge drinking at the bar in
the lounge on their first night, and
candyman was on the job. At length,
Sam and I talked of our process. Just
shutting down the obvious guy would
make a statement about the social
hazards of candy striping the college
kids. Or, a more complex approach was
to angle further upstream.

"We're in no hurry." I said. "So
let's do both."

"It might spook the horses but, we
could ask for a larger amount than
what's usually available at the bar."
she said.

"We should let animal instinct

work for us, not against us." I said.
"And whether they're nervous or not, a
burn's a burn. Our operational bar's
lower than a dealer's since our values
differ. Don't overdo it, just ask for
a bit more than is appropriate out of
hand for one sitting."

"Our values differ, yes." Sam
said. "But it may still be enough for
handcuffs, therefore, the man might
think that's what we want."

"Do we look like cops to you?" I
asked.

"Well, I don't think so. But,
what does that even mean?" she said.
"As far as I'm concerned, people either
are or aren't junkies. So, I think the
question is whether or not we look like
jonesers."

"Dangerous, sure, but not cops.
We come across as too close to the edit

for paid state agents." I said. "We think like them, it's true. We are citizens. But we tally far beyond our fair share of eccentricities for uniformed work."

"It's possible he's a freelancer, supplying himself." she said. "Which would mean he's political, and we get to bag two hats. A big bird with a small stone."

"The bartender hates him." I said. "He's not working alone though. The burly guy who sits by the door and never talks is a spotter."

"Either he's for us or against us, so they say." she said. "Maybe I shouldn't exceed the daily special on the deal, you know, we could still just grease everybody who fits the profile on our way out, and call it even."

"Alright. Let's ski a few more

days and see what happens."

twenty-five.

Sam befriended the candyman with
an approach that parted from our
typical moxy. We were on vacation,
after all, with plenty of time to test
new methodologies. In her healthy,
waxing zeal to be a peacemaker of the
cosmos, chumming it up with the
denizens of the bar and actually
drinking, she pulled off an act that
was one in a million. Her explanation
of me to them was, we were friends and
business partners not involved
romantically; I was a writer type, she
was my editor, and we'd come to ski.

I understood why she did it, but
her barfly character made the situation
more precarious than I preferred. She
was really hamming it up. At any rate,
the ruse was ensnaring both the silent

Denver Day

wingman and the point-of-sales man with
an offer that many people, particularly
cokeheads, can't refuse. She acted
with great gusto, comporting herself as
generally above the fray yet plausibly
dirty, an intellectual type, straight-
laced but letting loose on holiday
where no one knew her name. A ploy
rather close to the truth, in fact.

So she made friends with the guy,
and they were over there drinking
highballs and doing nailbumps. After
twenty-four hours of it, she put out
the bait: "Fuck me. Take me back to
your room. Bring your friend."

First walked the rover then out
Sam followed by the silent partner.
Fifteen minutes later she returned
alone to the lounge. I could tell by
the look in her eyes, our vacation was
at its conclusion.

"All done. Come see!" she said.

The bartender flashed us a grin as we made our way toward the door. Time can get real nonlinear in the presence of death and/or justice, when declarations like "thank you" or "come back anytime" are better made with the eyes than the mouth.

We walked the short distance to candyman's room. She'd opened their throats with a big kitchen knife, then put the two of them bloody naked and entangled on the bed, and covered them with a floral print comforter. Proud of her editorial flourish, she smiled at me widely.

"So how are ya?" I asked.

"Intoxicated. High as a kite. Blech." she said, swaying. "Quietude and green tea, please."

Thus I began triaging her side effects from the liquor and cocaine

Denver Day

use, and briefly we went back to our
room. Sam's account covered all of our
five minute cash-in with the hegemons
of sex and death on that day for sure.
After the brief but much welcome ass
sex, she was more clearheaded. Gently
we got the hell out of town.

     "They may only want to pin a medal
on us, I'm pretty sure that's the local
consensus, but we're not from here and
don't know the sheriff. I don't want
to be caught flatfooted if someone
comes looking for who snuffed the
wolfman's brother." she said. "Let's
go."

     So our citizenship prize from the
bartender would have to be awarded in
absentia. "I bet they'll love the
arrangement though." I said.

     We loaded the luggage, left the
room key on the nightstand, and began
an all-night drive back to Denver. I

had the sudden notion that Jules preferred avoiding unnecessary, ex post facto artistic statements with corpses. It was just her opinion, not a censure.

twenty-four.

As you might imagine, that drive back to Denver is narrow often and winding, not unpleasant but dark at night. I did all the driving and Sam was juiced enough to keep us both up. With her blood chemistry being what it was, I could understand why she was wearing sun-glasses despite the night.

"Rather indulgent of you, these past two days, yes?" I remarked.

"It was the only way I knew to get them both." said Sam. "Measures short of otherwise would've left that operation functionally intact."

Denver Day

"Your dedication's admirable. I can't immerse that "deeply" in the game. Has to do with my past, it would kill me. Hence, perhaps, my compensating for it with hardware." I said. "Are you coming down?"

"The blow makes me feel like a zombie whore." she said. "And the alcohol makes me feel retarded. That stuff's not indulgence, it's rat poison."

"Your choreography at the end was indulgent." I said. "In my opinion."

"Your opinion's important and it's a fair assessment. It certainly made me feel better." she said. Both ready for a long winter's nap, we got home at dawn and slept the clock around.

Back to our daily business, we'd not heard from Red since she'd left for the police academy in Fort Collins.

After work on our first night back, discussing the hegemons of marketplace economies, Sam and I speculated about Red's consideration of an actual badge.

"I don't see how it will help." I said.

"Yeah but I've known her for years. She just got bored and decided to add a useful credential." Sam said. "Chelsea Red knows a lot of cops but don't expect her to join the city force. She's worked as a private investigator for decades and focuses on private clients."

"Irish police work." I said.

"Is often thankless but somebody must, or someone else will. You're one to talk, anyway."

"As for my own labels, I'm only a journalist anymore insofar as I'm irretrievably embedded, and a P. I. only by sheer necessity." I said. "So what that actually makes me is an anonymous politician and a gonzo who writes a lot of stories about my long-winded tenure as an interstate dishwasher. I don't mean to sound hypocritical regarding Red's labels; I'm just thinking of the implications for us as a company because it's important that I, or we, remain philosophically relevant."

"Regardless of how come, what for, whither, and whence I trust it will be a good thing." said Sam. "A rolling stone gathers no moss."

Maybe Red's wayfaring would illuminate the path, and Sam was definitely right about rolling stones. The moral obligations of self-righteous, embedded dishwashers beget wanderlust. There was an undertow in Denver just like anywhere else, and I'd have to put it behind me eventually.

We made the best of our time that
spring. Our little precinct stayed
generally quiet and clean. The nightly
card playing at the diner persisted.
But in the back of my mind was an
interrogative upthrust, among the
layers of thought where Jules had
encountered the same question, which by
her dying she'd firmly answered. Her
prescription for us carried some
subjective bias since her cards had
already been called, but Jules' was a
clear model and it was worthy of
careful consideration.

twenty-three.

Apropos of Red's ongoing
educational activities, one ought never
discount the value of networking. When
she returned in March, she was even
more blue-eyed and full of piss, and

jumped right back into her routine at the Briton and with us. I and Sam selected a need-to-know policy about certain information and didn't tell her about the ski trip. We might've omitted that story even if she hadn't just come from the police academy. I'm sure she appreciated being spared, since possession is nine-tenths of the law. In certain respects, I knew it would be a little weirder to live and work with her, but she was still a roommate and a full partner in the venture.

Jules liked both Sam and Red but she was stumped seemingly, or perhaps indifferent regarding what my next move could be. As she became more accustomed to her death credential, my ground-floor patron was less hellbent anymore to the karma-police campaign. I still appreciated Jules' hanging around when she didn't have to, and that she had a kind of love for me that

had made a way for us to keep working
together. But again, even though I
wasn't dead yet, the way we were
fighting the individual battles was of
less philosophical consequence than I
preferred.

Jules never entertained macro-
cosmic delusions about why she did what
she did. Her motivation was self
respect, not grand and gratuitous
ideals of saving the world. In her
mind, the former relies strictly on the
latter. Any altruism in the philosophy
of Tex derived mainly from her
justifiable solipsism where enforcement
of her own dignity made good organic
karma. After all, it was I who'd
turned the whole operation into a
community service campaign, right?
Nevertheless, regardless of events
unfolding, we'd met the Baltimore trip
on her terms, and Jules continued to
have a strong hand in organizational
policy.

I wasn't, and still I am not, out to change the world at the expense of all other meritorious objectives. For one thing, I'd made new observations as already described, about the apparent net-zero improvement in the state of humanity, despite our theoretically infinite efforts at weeding out problematic characters. Also, because I know the world around us is the very definition of change, I realize going overly bananas against a natural flux, for any purpose beyond actual physical exercise, is a standard misappropriation of effort.

Right action can drastically change both the world and the agent of record. That's a funny thing about concentrated effort. Right effort, applied effectively, alters the ontology of, and for, the people involved. Therefore it's a key aspect of true growth. It's part of the recipe for effective success, and a practical example of dependent origination. It is entertaining that non-dualism results in a situation where one's efforts are concurrently both successful and unsuccessful.

Learning the consequences of right action is important for anyone and was a big deal to me. New growth in my world perspective began with Jules and was still occurring, and my affairs had become truly adventurous.

Philosophical mastery also has sociological bearing but in America, the liberty which accompanies enlightened thought can outshine common public policy, or occlude itself, which hinders the marketing of applied philosophy at an institutional level. Light seems to cast shadows.

On the subject of marketing, if the waters were already properly

chummed up through elimination of
cocaine and heroin dealers (and one
politician / businessman, so far),
then what new and interesting options
naturally might follow? As a
historical woman, friend of mine, and
quick spirit, Jules' patronage was
making me more effective, for sure.
And Red's and Sam's contributions
weren't anything to sneeze at either.
So whatever the new plan turned out to
be, I knew the team would be
formidable. But, as is typical of
relationships with the truth, it's fair
to say the answer to questions of
"what's really next" changed like
weather.

twenty-two.

Some weeks after Red's return from
Fort Collins she visited me on a night
shift at the Briton regarding a job
over in Boulder. It was a short road

trip, relatively local. The object was shutting down some nightclub supplier. Incidental to the ambient cottage industry of vice that shadows university campuses, some operation was getting local college kids dirty, and had gotten itself made by Boulder County authorities who'd run out of patience.

With a little creativity, the immense demand for cocaine can be incorporated into the safety protocols of these jobs, but that sword cuts both ways as burns are always a possibility despite common ground. Boulder was scripted to end like all our other details, but the presentation would be different. Namely, the deviation was, we were in the shoes of neither buyer nor seller. We'd just be road agents, outright highwaymen, and some of the element of surprise was lacking because we wouldn't be a principal party to the drug deal. Alternatively, it could be said the approach relied entirely on surprise, with our busting in like the Kool-Aid Man.

Outside of police operations and the rank of hazards due to general unpredictability among drug traffickers, I personally think people are less likely to expect a burn from sellers. Then again, Jules was killed as a seller, right after burning the buyers, but maybe I was over-thinking the matter. After all, the politician job had gone smoothly with its new approach, right? That night at the diner, in the absence of Red who was gathering up sleep for the next day's first shift, Sam voiced her general optimism and cautious skepticism.

"How do we know everybody on the wrong end of the gun deserves to be there?" she asked. "When we're involved with the deal, we know in our minds that we're not really there for

the stated purpose of buying or selling
dope. On those jobs we're there to
witness the other party's explicit
involvement, then shut 'em down. And
we're never there to burn ourselves.
These potentials always weigh heavily
in our risk mitigation."

"Anything can be second-guessed,
you know." I said. "We could be
deployed to burn an undercover agent.
Or the set-up could be on us.
Theoretically."

"Anything can be soft-pedaled too.
There's always risk, yes." Sam said.
"I suppose we think of it like any
other job on such terms: You might get
shot, but probably not, so good luck.
Full stop."

She was right about that. I
considered the relationship between
changes in methodology and right
action. Though it was a far cry from

Tex versus the barista, by that point I could make a strong argument for a standing army and an executive seal. Theoretically.

twenty-one.

Working alone is useful for standing personal ground and clear political speech. Advocates of solo work will tell you it's cleaner forensically, that less complexity means less entropy. Alternatively, the incorporation of civil infrastructure is the very definition of plurality, and therefore, of partisanry. So if an institution means to preserve the rigor and purity of its standards at the individual level among its membership, then organizational constituency must be exclusively and uniformly of one mind pursuant to the group's actionable philosophy.

Eventually, adding people to a situation leads to a state of entropy beyond hope of exact, subtle control. Some stop-gap entropy management methods exist such as, for example, a working internal census, but the only census I was keeping could be tallied on one hand. It was the job of some ad hoc committee of which I was now a de facto member to run the organizational census among the greater logistical network to which we were subscribed. I grew increasingly concerned that responsibility for the operations and maintenance of the political machinery is a job inherited by people who have stayed in one place too long.

In light of the foregoing assessments of the body politic, maybe Red's new credential and affiliation with the state of Colorado's law enforcement community was just the sort of partisan exercise our organization needed. Repeatedly, Sam had professed certainty that it wouldn't change Red's nature as an operator, but I didn't buy that story for one hot minute.

Back to the Boulder job, I'd expected some sort of open-air scenario where we'd be picking off marked buyers and sellers with rifles. Instead, the instructions detailed a risky ambush in the back office of a nightclub at peak operating hours. Barging in during a transaction in progress is dangerous. But on the other hand, if properly arranged, the plan did reduce our chances of being set up. Mr. Marion supplied us with three clean nine-millimeter semiautomatic pistols and tactical clips.

The arrangement was for eleven o'clock on a mid-April Friday night. The day of the job, we loaded ourselves and our gear into my car and drove out to Boulder. Red directed us to a booth by a window at a café diner in the university's merchant district.

"We'll go in and mow down every last asshole in the room." said Red. "No words, no winks, no nothing but hot lead. There should be some half dozen of them. Even if they're armed, it should still be a piece of cake."

"They might have a watch posted, like with a weapon trained on the door." I said.

"That's a risk yeah." she said. "Any lookout like that is number one, obviously."

We spent the afternoon engaging local co-eds and other vegetarian delicacies. Around dinnertime we checked into a hotel, rested, and showered ourselves into readiness for our night out.

When we came on location at ten,

the wet bar was already about a brisk business. We ordered chemical tools, occupied an open nook, and after ten minutes of scenery, Sam took a spin on the dance floor.

"Doesn't it take you back?" I said. "It has been thousands of years since I was inside one of these joints."

"Look there, one of our buddies." said Red, nodding toward the bar. A white male of medium build with short dark hair gelled slick back, wearing a gray shirt and black trousers, was in a convo with the bartender.

twenty.

As that night's moment of truth approached, despite the many unknowns, we were feeling pretty good about the job. Seeing the poor caliber of people

in the club made the effort seem
pettier. Slick hardware in the belt is
always reassuring too. The first guy
finished his chat with the bartender
and took his drink through a door
painted the same color as the wall.

That was our door too, Red said.
"We'll walk back there at exactly
eleven by my watch. There's another
door in the room, we'll use that one to
get out of the building. The deal
won't take longer than three minutes,
hence our operational window. But I
expect it will take us half that long,
at most.

Ten thirty came. Sam returned
from the dance floor. Patiently we
ticked like clocks. Our seller in the
gray shirt returned to the bar for
another exchange with the barkeep, this
time with the addition of another dude
in turquoise parachute pants and a
turban.

Denver Day

"What a way to go." Red said,
after the couple went back through the
blue door.

"Color's important." said Sam. I
tried to remember when I'd last worn
parachute pants.

Twenty minutes later, three
characters walked up and talked with
the same barman. They were the real
thing too, evidently. One was a wiry
looking black man with long slick
braids. Another was heavy set, a
brown-skinned male with a slick shaved
head. The third was a darkly tanned
female wearing all black no-bullshit
leather. These three were far more
dangerous-looking than the two who had
preceded them. The head count stopped
at five people who we would bring to a
halt within ten short minutes. The
trio ordered neat scotches and lingered
for five minutes at the bar. By my

watch, it was ten-fifty-seven when they went through our blue door.

"There's a restroom back there. I'll go that way now." Red said. "Come on in two minutes. It's a public toilet but the bartender might have an eye on that door, so act cool."

I looked at my watch, then leaned over to give Sam's epiglottis a squeeze with my tongue. Along with hooking up, dancing, or shooting people, making out is one of the most logical things to do at nightclubs. We kept that up for a half minute. Before our entering the blue door, we went and leaned on the increasingly crowded bar for a few moments as if momentarily opting for a quick piss before making our next drink purchase. We slithered through the egress with a giggle, playing the part of giddy casual lovers hand-in-hand, without looking back. Within moments, we'd be finished and through the back

door. For sure it'd be noisy, and we
didn't have silencers, but odd gunshots
mixed with loud house music is a
popular motif.

The hall turned right, back in the
direction of the bar. We saw the
restroom door, from which Red then
emerged. The corridor was empty but
for us. Above a closed door on the
left wall a blue neon sign hung,
halfway between the toilet door and the
turn in the corridor behind us. The
prevailing ambiance was dimness, but
the neon blue subtly heightened
visibility.

Eleven o'clock struck. I readied
my heater and the partners did the
same, bidding farewell to the luxuries
of hesitation and do-overs. Gently,
Red tried the door knob, which was
locked. Rather than shooting the lock,
we'd kick in the flimsy door, which was
still going to cost us a few precious

moments of suspended disbelief. Red was reading my mind.

"Kick it open on three. Once it's cleared, come on with the hot lead." she whispered. "One two three."

After one solid kick to the right of the handle, that door came right open and we started cooking.

nineteen.

As the door kicker, my gun play was delayed. By the time I opened fire, several of our targets had already taken lead from Sam and Red, and were down. That's dangerous of course, because they're low and it's uncertain if they're still hot. So since we were prevailing handily, I rained bullets on those wild cards for insurance. The guy in the gray shirt and the heavyset bald dude were the first to hit the ground. The female in leather took a knee, although she did not appear to have taken a hit during the initial strafing, so I hosed her down before re-ventilating the two first fallen. Her neutralization was reassuring since she was probably their most significant combat asset.

The crazy-eyed guy with the weave also might have been capable of presenting somewhat of a bother. He and the dude in the parachute pants got the business from us simultaneously, and were the last to go down. Following that, quickly, everyone received a final dealbreaker to the cranium. And that was all she wrote. From the first bullet to the last, the assault took ten seconds, tops. None of them fired a shot.

As part of our standard signature (notwithstanding the facts of life in Crested Butte) we left the mess

perfectly intact and we didn't stick
around to accommodate further extra
credit or philosophical inquiry. Red
pointed at our back door and out of it
we walked, upright but wary. We
encountered not even an alley cat in
the rear lot. In a half minute we were
at the car and beginning our return
commute to Denver.

"I was having funny feelings about
this one." Sam reiterated. "But it
was alright."

Traffic was light at that hour.
Once back in Denver, we returned to our
diner. Before getting out of the car
in the diner parking lot, we executed a
quick, spicy, three-way fluid exchange
in the backseat, at the pleasures of
the hegemons of sex and death.

Like Sam, regarding the Boulder
detail I'd also felt some foreboding,
but of course we'd talked about it and

Denver Day

done our best to secularize our
premonitions. Test pilots experience
such butterflies before some flights,
but it never means certain doom. I'd
been concerned someone of us might take
a hit during the deal, due to the wild
west nature of the operation. But
maybe it wasn't a false positive, so
driving back I was wondering, what if
we were sensing legitimate warnings but
had misidentified the context?

Red's new badge was still a shiny
object of fixation in my mind, because
of the political gamble it presented to
our operation. Before, our oversight
had stopped with the hegemons of sex
and death, and had gone no further than
our own logistical draft. However,
beyond my recent personal advances in
politics and applied altruism, as I've
discussed at some length, now one of us
had added an additional guild standard
whose institutional face explicitly
denotes obligations to the public.

260

That isn't necessarily a bad
thing, I mean, theoretically it could
be helpful. In fact, the obligation to
fellow citizens is encompassed, daresay
enshrined, in our political will as a
matter of postmodern political science.
However, because of the phenomenon of
epistemic feedback, whether it's the
Dark Ages or tomorrow, it does matter
who's involved, even if they're aloof.

eighteen.

By that point in the business day,
subconsciously I'd expected to be
dealing with either my own death or one
of my partner's. I've always felt the
déjà vu sensation psychologically
pleasant like being rewarded with extra
leisure time after a successful ordeal.
I was feeling that way after Boulder.

One tractable interpretation of

the abundant second-guessing and funny
feelings, was we'd defied a fated
failure on the Boulder job. Beating
the odds in a group effort and doing so
alone are widely different tasks.
Either way, historically, consequent
change in the universe must be
accounted for, to keep true victories
from being rewarded with bondage or
death. Countless accountabilities come
to mind, in fact, but proper
documentation is important.

Regarding the subjectivity of our
world, the conversation here shines on
a certain set of facts of human nature
and the law of the sea. I may come off
as a nihilist, but again we find
evidence that a certain many things
necessarily don't matter as much as one
might have believed. It might be more
accurate to say things don't matter as
much as they once did, but that's a
subjective assessment. Maybe it's
better considered as an observation of

one's own agency making the world less heavy, rather than any discovery of the world's meaninglessness.

For example, it might matter differently for the people we mowed down at the nightclub. Like, did they enjoy the same type of return to forever as Jules? When people die without proper preparation, I suspect they're just dead fucks, full stop, forever. The terms of hegemons vary where universal principles may not. If we had been burned down in Boulder, it wouldn't really matter because we'd live on anyway. For the likes of Sam, Red, me, and Jules, among the infinite manifestation of our souls, that's only a new birth of sorts.

The people we killed that night were either unenlightened dead or they aren't. Maybe they did outshoot us, but we outshined their whole universe short-lived as it was, altering fate in

our favor. Such efficacy in agency
illustrates the importance of merit
among oneself, one's contemporaries,
and among all who've ever lived and
ever will. That describes a crowded
house because there's no acceptance
without merit, time out of mind.
Houses lacking merit aren't homes. If
encountering a scenario where oneself
appears to be the only agent of a free
will, perhaps one ought to operate
nevertheless, as if all deeds were
under review by meritorious progenitors
and progeny, regardless of whether one
is indulged with contemporaries.

We thought we'd averted a bad
situation with our collective agency.
We thought wrong. The state agents
entered the diner in the same moment
that I noticed a man in plainclothes
fingering us through the front window.
Any other day, I might not have
realized the ones entering the diner
were special, but under the

circumstances I knew. The person on
the sidewalk had called down hell on
us, I understood. I also knew if I
didn't settle the matter right then,
he'd skate and I wouldn't get another
chance to do the job right. Someone
else might make him pay, another place,
some other time, in a different
context. But for the two of us, that
was the moment.

I don't know who he was, but he
was fucked. Despite what was soon to
happen, and even if I lost my freedom,
I still held the moral high ground.
The finger man remained on the
sidewalk, sticking around to watch the
collar, and the agents closed on our
table, hands on their weapons. If you
know anything of felony arrests, then
you know those detectives weren't in a
tea-and-cookies frame of mind.

From my belt holster I pulled the
forty-five, and quickly put two hollow-

point slugs through the diner window
into the guy on the porch. Down he
went. The last thing I remember was
hearing more shots, but they weren't
coming from me. Next, I was either
dead or unconscious, although based on
the lack of clarity I was experiencing
and the absence of all enlightened
beings, I had a hunch that I was alive
and unconscious.

seventeen.

Instances of the incommunicado
detention, virtual or otherwise, of
American journalists notwithstanding:
For decades, I've kept a mindfulness
practice respecting incarceration, to
cultivate a peace of mind that prevents
removal of my free will and serenity by
means of kidnapping or imprisonment.
The practice is comparable to keeping a
valid passport at the ready despite
having no plans for international

travel.

Such a practice also leads to heightened sensitivity about the predicaments of incarcerated people. A class imprisoned and without basic civil liberties is a foundation of traditional "civilization" and most people aren't objectively or consciously aware of it. (It's a particular type of fishtank despotism). For example, "establishment" society depends on the subjugation of an expendable class in order to keep up its "superiority." Point being it's a sad state of affairs and a devastating impeachment of its champions, and enough to warrant a legal name change for one who comes to learn the folly and complicity of their predecessors.

I don't mean to say actual criminals shouldn't be managed until they're successfully rehabilitated, but for every individual evil asshole

avoiding incarceration there are a
thousand people in American prisons who
could cite bad social economics not
criminal justice as the first principle
of their situation. Don't like the
theory from the perspective of social
science? Biology renders the same
verdict; I challenge you to research
relationships, between incarceration
and the teleology of modern humanity's
evolution, and you should be moved at
what you discover.

A common currency exists among
imprisoned or otherwise oppressed
populations, and even among those who
only study such institutions or
advocate for their constituencies.
That's part of the "religion" of the
judiciary. Remaining mindful
constantly, regarding any and all
beings imprisoned, lost, enslaved, or
otherwise bonded in separation from
their home at heart, means always
carrying extra baggage. When such

baggage is recognized, and sometimes reacted to negatively in contexts presumed to be apart from institutions of bondage, one can see aspects of society which rely on the existence of abjection or its implementation without due cause. Classist arguments may make citation of some cause or another, but the sociological phenomenon of arbitrary entitlement to classes underfoot, for which there is clearly no good cause, is easily observable nevertheless. Oppressing those who contribute to such bondage through bad faith or ignorance is the realm of natural law, the quicker the better.

With a little caution, carrying some extra baggage on behalf of strangers at all times is a winning idea in the sense that eventually, every being becomes liberated whenever a "last cop out" situation occurs in the universe. Also, if one happens to become imprisoned, or a contemplative monastic, or manages to get compromised or restrained somehow otherwise, then the psychological groundwork is already in place for accomplishing certain aspects of the ordeal. Because of the practical and generally predictive accountability of altruism among whitelisted mariners, and their tacit awareness of the greater organic cause and effect, the practice has been a maritime custom time out of mind. It may not always be pretty, but in my mind it's good insurance in this fallen, odd, haunted, robot graveyard full of prisons, hungry ghosts, body thieves, and bondsmen.

So when I woke up in a hospital bed, I had the sudden notion that my mindfulness practice for incarcerated people was about to get a rigorous field trial. Jamais vu before beginning to recollect recent events and realizing my location, I was mystified regarding my status. First,

I remembered shooting the guy at the diner. Next, the Boulder nightclub came back, then I recalled I'd probably been shot hence the noteworthiness of my being alive. Following that thought was recollection of sex with Red and Sam in the diner parking lot. And now, there I was, in some hospital bed.

Because I've been criticized as being overly philosophical, I made a concerted effort to take the situation seriously, if not for my own sake then for the analytical reasons. I was definitely in the belly of a beast, there were slippery slopes at every turn. A moment later, a nurse came in with a few grouchy answers for me, but first a question:

"Do you know why you're here?"

"Yes, it seems that I have been shot. Is that correct?"

Denver Day

"Yes. You have suffered two
bullet wounds, one in the back of your
left hand and one in the upper left
thigh. Nine millimeter rounds. You
will make a full physical recovery.
Additionally, you are in the custody of
the Colorado State Police who say an
arraignment and bond hearing will be
docketed now that you're out of
surgery, lucid, and recovering."

Changing the subject, I was asked
if I was hungry, thirsty, or needed to
use the restroom. All three, yes, I
answered. The nurse nodded and left
the room for a minute, returning with a
pair of crutches. I walked to a toilet
down the hall, where I relieved myself
gratefully.

Because of security implications
for both myself and the nurse, I didn't
ask where exactly I was, address-wise.
For similar reasons, I didn't query
under which statute I'd be charged.

But I knew I probably wasn't far from
my own condo and I had a fair idea
which of my actions were of material
interest to the law. There were also
concerns of Red's and Sam's current
civil status, and of disclosing certain
historical facts unnecessarily. I
wanted to be careful of digging myself,
or them, any deeper.

The nurse returned with my food
and asked me if I wished to speak with
a state police investigator that
evening or if I'd rather wait until
morning.

"I'll wait."

I checked out my food, then
explained my vegan diet, so the tray
was removed. Ten minutes later, a
plate of fresh fruit arrived.

I wondered if my partners were
also shot, but I doubted it since I was

the only active civilian shooter in the
diner. Judging by the non-lethal
locations of my own wounds, my shooters
were well-suited to their peaceable
vocation. I was fairly confident that
my target never got up again, of
course. Sam and Red probably didn't
break leather, they probably weren't
injured, and possibly weren't charged,
but they could have been picked up for
the Boulder detail which I suspected
was the origin of the demised
plainclothed informant.

sixteen.

     First thing come morning when I
opened my eyes, there was a slick dick
in the room, the perfect lizard with
electric black eyes, giving me an
eyeballing as stand-out as any.
Impressively inert. A gaping maw. The
detective was all dicks, elbows,
thumbs, knuckles, and broomsticks. I

definitely sensed reasonability but no
tolerance for bullshit. This character
was a windfall, so I didn't open.
Willingly enough, the detective did.

"We have a body, Rick. And a
roomful of people including three state
police investigators who saw you do it.
Colorado Revised Statue says you will
answer for it as a matter of criminal
procedure."

I just played it straight. "That
guy was part of a cocaine syndicate
that's been tabling at nightclubs in
Boulder. His leading you to me was an
effort at causing your agency to work
in the best interest of that criminal
enterprise, and against the people of
the state of Colorado. That's the
truth, tell me if I'm wrong."

The detective glanced at the floor
then swept me with a drafting gaze.
"Is that exactly what you would say to

a judge?"

"Let's have the governor swear me in."

"We don't need the governor for that. Pending the full facts, this discussion might be ex post facto. Let me say this to you, Mr. Thompson. I am your best friend because we share some common ground. I am the principal investigator of this homicide. And if your information is true and legal, there won't even be a grand jury."

Rarely does anyone use or even know my last name. I rarely give it out. But he had it.

"Think on it. I'll be back tonight." The detective walked out sideways.

Nobody had mentioned Red's or Sam's name out loud, but the subject

was pressed tacitly. I'd sit there all
day while that brown-shirted ectotherm
checked out my story. Which was a true
story, in both its spoken and unspoken
ways. I'd committed no felony, such is
the nature of ethical work.

Depending on the results of that
day's intensive background check into
me, the detective could either have me
prosecuted for murder and even as a
serial killer, or, let me go outright.
Relying on blind faith in other
individuals is dicey, and this was a
textbook example of having to do just
exactly that, but I'd given the ugly
truth readily and affirmation of my
story could be located easily and
quickly by my investigator. I thought
of Red's new credential again and of
the law enforcement community
generally. Again I wondered if they
were sitting in the clink, if they'd
been arraigned, or if they'd even been
picked up at all.

I'd mentioned the nightclub but didn't go any further because it was off topic, deeper into foul territory. Of all people, my detective would respect, hopefully, the occupational necessity for me to draw the line there. It can all go without saying, that by rights, for me and people who think like me, the traffic stop in Boulder stood on its own merit and legitimized my actions in the diner. The diner mess simply was what it was, regardless of whether the matter ultimately downshifted me and my muse into the Colorado Department of Corrections. Another option of the moment, of course, was for me to disappear myself from that hospital.

fifteen.

I didn't want to accidentally close any bad deals or slam any doors by talking out of school to the medical corps. Because for the moment all options were on the table, so I and that nurse continued our minimalist conversation. I did sweet-talk my way into a vegan breakfast delivered from off campus, but there was no talk of firearms, police, narcotics inter-diction, nightclubs, court, ethics, the future, the past, the dead, or the weather much.

During supper, slick the dick returned, and again I let the conversation come to me, since I wasn't holding all proper cards. Unless the game is something like solitaire, nobody ever has all the cards. But I knew damn well the obvious. Some contingencies are stronger than others but we both knew it would be real easy to throw the book at me. The agent paused, either thinking or feigning contemplation.

Denver Day

Mine were real bullets during the
event of so much late interest to the
Colorado State Police. So were the
ones in the sidearm of the detective,
who didn't come right out and say it,
but I was gonna skate. The identity of
the guy I shot mattered. Another key
in my favor was that the detective
understood the law. For that I was
lucky. Eo ipso justice contrived
describes some lack of justice; karma
is blind and duplicitous insofar as
it's real, ipso facto.

"The guy you shot at the diner is
dirty. Was. Very. The homicide was
justifiable under the circumstances. A
panel hearing of the law enforcement
standards regulatory body of the state
of Colorado will be convened after the
fact. Regarding this matter you will
be asked to give a brief verbal
statement to the panel, and that will
be all. I'll be in touch."

Five minutes passed before any more words were spoken. Of course neither my forty-five nor Marion's nine-millimeter were with me any longer, and I was wondering if my car was still parked at the diner where Red and Sam and I had left it with fogged-up windows. Red and Sam.

"Was anyone else brought in?"

"No." He walked out. I never caught his name.

Fifteen minutes later, a different nurse came in with a cardboard box of my personal effects (minus the handguns). She explained to me the technical aspects of my two wounds and their maintenance, and told me I was free to go whenever I felt like it. One hour later I got up, dressed, took the crutches, walked past the restrooms to the elevator, and rode down to the lobby. Outside I was met with snowfall

and hailed a cab to our condo. I never
saw my forty-five again.

   No one was home. I showered off
the strata of weird shit collecting on
me from road trip to co-ed café to
nightclub job to car sex to diner
shootings to hospital plume to cab
ride. The time was eight in the
evening and I felt a strange fatigue
where my head was tired and my body was
drowsy but I wasn't sleepy. I pondered
the irony of my present return to the
diner and how jarring it might be for
patrons who witnessed the shooting to
see me returned. They'd just have to
suck it up. I put on my fluffy plaid
pajamas and boiled some tea, first
things first. I'd wait and deal with
the world whenever anyone came home
from wherever they were, which was
probably work. No big rush.

   I thought of Jules again. Might
she be critical of my recent lack of

subtlety? That crazy Old West bullshit at the nightclub, which led the footman to the diner, was of Red's hatching not mine, after all. As an old friend used to say when very bad things befell others, "it was probably just a big misunderstanding."

fourteen.

My roommates woke me at four a.m., having buffed the scent of diner and pub from their own hides, donned favorite pajamas, and joined me in bed. Like fairly well-behaved adults, we rested gratefully and quietly.

It was an optimistic thing for us to have been returned intact, to one another, in short order, with such minor hassle. It was hopeful in that sometimes life's dramas unfold artfully, as they ought, and that protagonists don't always lose in real

life to end up in prison while rats
rule the world and enjoy its finer
aspects. It's a victory when the
applied rule of law accommodates
natural justice, spirit, liberty, and
friendship.

That my present state of freedom
resulted from enlightened right action
by a state agent of justice was not a
bad thing, though I felt a naïve guilt
for being surprised when things worked
out correctly. I called it a sea
change with deep implications. Sam and
Red also felt the same not-unpleasant
shock to the conscience. I pondered
the extent to which I was obligated to
the good detective, not in his state
agency (I knew the answer to that),
but as an individual. The answer soon
set upon me, as obligations to any
facet of the dharma are equal.

Sprung, the next day I was back at
the Briton, second shift, with my

wounded hand in a wrap. I used a cane
for a week. To have hidden would've
been to assert liability for something
which even by official accounting was
simply a legitimate unfolding of the
law of the sea.

Unlike actions of intellectual
dependency, acts of free will are
executed on ethically stable but
politically unpopular grounds of merit,
and they usually violate reasonable
thresholds of safety by standards of
the general public. It follows that
the notion of safety is widely
misunderstood. Crowds are cowards, so
goes mob rule.

Beyond my vantages and those of
public eyes, old friends, or the
hegemons', my position at the time
created a political historical drag.
Twenty years from now, someone could
decide to bring action against me, far
and away from the facts and people

involved with the homicide as it was
duly and justly executed and disposed.
This loose end and ones like it can
color the context of people's
existences.

Loose ends have ongoing
teleological presence in a life,
begging questions of privacy and
natural rights. All rights are a right
to privacy habeas corpus. Within
affairs of state or without, the
epistemic feedback which accompanies
surveillance has drastic influences.
In fact, active surveillance,
clandestine or otherwise easily amounts
to total ownership and psychological
control. Bondage, a high crime of the
realm. Somehow, my mind felt like a
vessel boarded by potentially friendly
but incredibly dangerous pirates.

thirteen.

Hipster Bricks

On the second day after my
release, the three of us worked night
shift and met at the diner afterward
for our usual playing gin, sketching,
scheming onto paper napkins, and
holding court with other nighthawks.
Regularly we offered to Sam that we go
to the Briton instead, for the sake of
her getting a change in scenery, and
she always refused. Too many drunks
there, she always said.

Let me tell you, that night we had
perplexed looks belying tip-of-the-
tongue questions, like, why wasn't I in
jail? and, can I also get away with
cold-blooded murder in a crowded diner?
and, may I see your bullet holes?
among other farcical interrogative
shits. The wound on my thigh was
interesting to behold and the one on my
hand was a darling also. Of course, I
didn't know the name of, or even see
the surgeon who'd patched me up.

Denver Day

We enjoyed the green tea and
mushroom tomato soup, and watched a
late snow through the new front glass
of the diner. No further shitbird
darkened the door for having misled
headmen to us.

The atmosphere in the diner had a
certain subtly cautious feel, as one
might expect after a calculated
political victory or prejudiced
termination. I say, all-night diner
people share more positive common
ground than all-night saloon people and
it was a sympathetic room. Still,
despite all of the many quizzical
glances, no one flat-out asked exactly
how I'd come to be sitting in a state
of wide-open-beaver freedom, in the
same room where three days past I'd
presented a heat-of-the-moment killing
so facile and boldfaced as to inspire
deep personal change in numerous
eyewitnesses. It probably would have
been fine to whistle past the

graveyard, had anyone pressed the issue
explicitly, but no one did. It
would've been gratuitous anyway.

Our company's operation still
derived from, although it was now
orders of measure different, than the
pattern of thought and operation to
which Jules had originally hipped me.
Any political victory beyond a personal
level, again, was not the original
purpose of our pursuits. But the
running series of events had aligned
our interests with those of others, in
spite of the facts of life regarding
spirit, liberty, intellectual
dependency, free will, and
organizational politics in their
juxtaposition with natural law and
social economy.

In any case, our actions were of
an incidental benefit to the common-
wealth. By some roundabout means we'd
become politicians and I've said that

Denver Day

before. The reality of political
agency never is as one might've
previously imagined, which for me could
be because I'd never seriously
considered a political career before,
and then when I did get involved, it
was without premeditation.

An alternate theory was, the
hegemons of sex and death had gotten
bored with the game and upped our
auntie. By definition, the hegemons
that I recognize don't do foolish, ill-
conceived things therefore maybe other,
interloping hegemons had caused some
disturbance in the eschatology. Maybe
Jules was the token interloper. Since
nothing truly matters anyway, was she
running a battery of digital philosophy
tests on us? Had she made some
observation from her enlightened
vantage that drove her to engineer
these events? Questions. I was full
of 'em.

It was probably time for us to get
new tattoos again, we decided. I took
on another face card, The Hanged Man
this time, who was wearing some really
nice trousers of motley. Sam added
more candy striping. Circumscribing
her ass hole, officer Red achieved a
little chattel ring, possibly the
absolute most attractive thing I'd ever
seen. Red's her own woman but horny
does as horny is.

twelve.

The morbidity (or non-dualistic
not-morbidity) of our situation
rarefied under my political lens.
Humankind are a self-reflective flora
manifesting around plasmatic celestial
bodies, thriving best when able to
purge or excrete our withered mass with
ease. Biologically, humanity is more
plantlike than many understand. We are
a seasonal plurality, a viral, hoary,

shiny creature whose object can suffer
badly but hasn't died because the tree
is too robust. The incessant death
confronting people on an "individual"
basis simply isn't death. Rather
philosophical death is only change.
Human civilization's subtle and fresh
incumbency, reminiscent of having
fought the law and won, is timely in
its coloration of "not-death" or
"death as a common misnomer."

   Case in point being Tex, who
managed to find the door to not-death
without political incorporation.
Hadn't she? She had in fact, if our
present disposition was that of her
constituent agency, which is what I
believed. Such was the brightline
test. In a room with one door and no
windows, the door's the only way?
Another option is never leaving, that's
possible at an institutional level.
Arguably and notwithstanding flexible
definitions of quantitative bounds,

staying in an empty room for a duration
of some infinite measure denotes actual
death, however. The concept of forever
is either a philosophical contradiction
or simply another brightline test for
the exclusivity of aliveness and
political agency.

Our haggling and wagering with the
hegemons of sex and death forced these
issues in my head. I'm lucky to
realize the odd combination of
emptiness and contingency among it all.
Since people fill their minds up with
shit that occludes nature, many
"individuals" are explicitly unaware
of the starkly vapid truth of the
world's naked gallows. Since being
shot in the head, Jules had been
farming-out knowledge in conflict with,
the predominance of implements and
rumors of death in the world. There's
no hurry for the likes of she and us,
coming or going. Time must be viewed
as strictly a tool, for the politics of

people and ontological hegemons.

All of this negation and meaninglessness really lubricated the motors on my mothership and brought to mind entertaining questions of what to do next. The efficacy of the will sustains unlimited questionability; yet, someone on the prowl for aesthetic experience can have it in abundance, even in something as inconsequential as a duplicitous quale or as baseless as unethical first principle.

Consider the altruism of Jules enforcing the karma of her individual mind and free will. Universally irrelevant? Yes, in multiple and good ways. But a novel aspect of the individually thriving beauty of her mind? Yes, aesthetics in cognition is a key for individual and collective existence, it prescribes living. In the local sense, regarding my little existential crisis after being shot, I

might again editorialize about the
river of life being a medium of
constant change, an understanding which
I consider to be part of the
philosopher's stone. This time the
veil was being pulled back further than
before. I was catching a fire in
Colorado.

Aesthetic justification mitigates
the nihilism that haunts empty rooms
which forever contain nothing but a
soul and a door. That's why Red, Sam,
Jules, I, and people like us are off
the secular grid. We have to be from
the get-go. Writing is a kind of
cognitive art, literature that is. As
a writer I realized long years ago,
creativity and beauty were one of the
fundamental meanings of life. Of
course, there are reasons for existence
besides lovemaking, gaming, eating, and
laughter.

More soup was ordered and slurped.

Denver Day

The conversation returned to
partisanship, where organizing the
faculties of one's present community is
key for more elaborate, nuanced, .
profound aesthetic, and for more
effective mastery. So having
accomplished a census, after what
fashion might we situate among the
dharma? We discussed.

Short minutes after declaring
there's no true death, and by the same
measure that not-death is also strictly
academic, then insisting none of it
matters anyway because dualism is a
basic logical fallacy, I've caught
myself here selling a strategy to
deliberately, rigorously map and
distribute individual essence and
wherewithal, in order to prevent
wasting any drop of our precious,
incoherent void.

eleven.

296

Late spring caught me in a protracted, easy convalescence. The Centennial State winter is nothing to sneeze at but its temperate season is magical. Despite our cool jobs and the heavenly weather, eventually we hit the road like a bolt of lightning. In case of retirement, disembodiment, or nostalgia, coming back to the diner and the Briton was a last-ditch option we could always rely on, we thought.

Besides tending to us, Jules spent much of her afterlife in Austin. Such is the haunt. There are lots of dead people in Austin. She also abides among the rocky, flaming, fundamental beauty of the infinite cosmological garden. In fact, hiding in weathered river stones for example, is how lost or wandering spirits get reborn inadvertently, like moths to flame becoming incorporated into some arbitrary life cycle. It happens.

Denver Day

We were discussing international
romping, patiently waiting for some
quorum of the muses to make known its
preference. Mexico's spaciousness,
proximity, and geopolitical relevance
to our agenda made it a good bet.
Probably neither Mexican nor American
officials would take issue with our
efforts to disrupt mega-methamphetamine
labs and heroin trafficking.

Hedging on stealth isn't a fool-
proof approach. Like our delicate
egress into this line of work in the
states, the use of caution would be
important when putting into the action
south of the border tambien. But the
narcotics cottage industry of capos,
dependents, and sister-wives is a
global concern. Such is political
corruption.

Distrito Federal was worth a trip
for teeth cleaning pro forma and Red

was fishing around for opportunities at fixing derelict paisanos in the Sierra Madres. We knew such jobs were in the offing.

"We can't take our art across so we'll need fresh hardware on the south side." Red said.

"Gunpowder isn't the only game in town." I said. "Piano string is quieter than firearms, for example."

"I think we should stick to what we know." she said. "Cars and guns."

We were free to go and be cool, according to absolutely no one who'd actually fess up to green-lighting us. For starters, our plan would put us in Ciudad de México to polish our idioms, improve our tans, and get proper sand in our underwear before confronting the chupacabra.

ten.

The currency's a tool, not an end unto itself. Profiteering's a kind of racketeering and it's a crime. But it could be said the buck stops short of the big game pursuant to the gamelike nature of the universe. Strictly business, the dollar's no joke. Because it doesn't have to be. People gathering up as much of it as they can in a game to see who can gather the most, is comparable to plumbers hoarding wrenches. Is hoarding wrenches practical for plumbers or plumbing? No, but wrench hoarding is a game that can be played. Capitalism is a game that's not inherently bad, but it's bad if the people freezing up the capital are bad. For argument's sake, one might divide the citizens of the world into two groups: people who restrict access to resources in bad faith, and those who do not.

Arrange a lucrative international narcotics black market around this turpitudinous trait of the universe's more ethically adrift denizens, and the result is a shitshow of cosmic breadth. Legal tender for debts public and private, the dollar serves as a public account ledger for trading both legally sanctioned coffee and black market cocaine. Oh yes, gram per gram, one's a paradigm shift stronger than the other, but the weaker, more enduring addiction is important too. At any rate, duplicitous institutional policy, equivocating between two different stimulant-producing crops, makes a two-headed monster of the dollar. American market presence follows suit as the dollar represents citizens' executive vesting. We must take back the night, so to speak, when it comes to our own political institutions. Or I must. I'm referring to more than just the "War on Drugs" policy.

Denver Day

A given region can have more
disparate socioeconomic situations than
others, so local definitions of upper
class or middle class are culturally
relative and various. Problems persist
with poverty in all urban areas, while
there remains much simple pastoral
rural living on all continents. But
the ruling class throughout the
Americas comprises a tiny fraction of
the general human population, pursuant
to the strata of global caste. Such is
the case in South American countries,
just as it is in the United States.

At the cost of the working class,
to include the working middle class, a
bourgeois oligarchy fights to retain a
monopoly on the means of production, or
the means of finance where there's no
production, or the military when
there's nothing to leverage except the
political will of a minority (which is
why history repeats itself mercilessly

for the unethical and small-minded).
The means of cocaine production is so
universally influential, for example,
that it can and often has served as a
trump to mitigate or reverse political
defeats suffered by such oligarchy.
Abjection, cocaine, prostitutes, and
old money, wow. Who's really who, or
which is which? Got political
troubles? Go hide in a coca tree.

Demand's hot everywhere, led by
the global West and a great supply is
produced on the southerly continent.
Unlike cocaine, the dollar's not
necessarily a commodity, capitally or
exclusively. In financial markets its
tenderability is hedged upon and
marketed, yes. Notwithstanding the
importance of philosophical guaranty,
however, it's only paper money.
Ironically the dollar is the universal
symbol of the South American cocaine
crop. What's worse, the dollar's
fundamental hedging on cocaine isn't

accidental at the U.S. foreign (and
domestic) policy level. It's legally
prescriptive of, but not representative
of my or my compatriots political will.
Hence, U.S. foreign policy's serving
primarily the political interests of
the galactic cocaine market is a
principal conflict of interest. Must I
spell it out? Either get off, or I'll
declare this nation to be forcibly
occupied.

I don't wish to proselytize on
moral grounds against drug use or the
natural libertarian right for honest,
peaceable people to go unmolested by
narcotics officers. But one of the
main reasons my drug use became so
terribly out of hand as a teenager is
because I was a teenager. Point being,
constant roaring black market
solicitation of young people and at-
risk youth particularly, is backed by
the dollar. And if my foreign policy
props it up, how can domestic policy be

effective to the contrary? In light of
foreign policy supporting the cocaine
crop de facto, the U.S. War on Drugs
public relations campaign is a farce as
big as the two-party political system
or the corporate-owned news media.
These farces have colossal body counts,
ever accumulating in the name of all
citizens. That's what happens when
people commit crimes in your name.
Well no shit, everybody in the universe
enjoys coke, especially babies.

The wrong kind of foreign
interests are vested in the dollar, and
they're all taking a whiff on Rick the
Rooster. Toward that end, why should
the people of the United States have to
suffer a debauched currency, among
other very bad things? It's an obvious
problem and nobody seems to give a
shit, which is why I, Sam, and Red went
south. Our challenges would include
staying on task and avoiding unwitting
defection, and I didn't think we were

much of a risk for going over to the dark side. Well, maybe Red, since she had the best credential for it.

The whole geopolitical narcotics industry could be made-up reality television, and I'm sure that's correct to some limited extent. But insofar as it's truly mismanaged as described, then it's a real problem, and I know there's a sufficient amount of stupid unfortunate truth to the story. And wherever the storyline may only be artifice, it's still marketing. Catch a college kid, not too young but just right, and the market gains a lifetime user and petty dealer whose individual market action justifies every failed recruiting effort to date.

Old money says "that's how it is. That's how it's always been. Anyway, what do we care?" New money says "let's do some blow." The devil hiding in the details says "money talks."

Well bullshit. We booked a direct
flight from Denver to Mexico City
traveling light with a purpose, doing
our part as citizens of the universe to
preserve the peace as best we could.
It might appear to have been also for
cheap thrills. I don't really know
what to say about that, if you must
ask. Maybe the world needs horses'
asses too. For ethical high ground,
motives simply are what they are.

The mid-May departure was financed
by dollars of course, and don't think
for a minute I wasn't keeping track of
them. Ultimately, they're all
philosophical dollars and they're mine.

"Do you think we'll end up in a
mass grave?" Sam pondered as our
flight boarded.

"Would it matter?" Red answered.

Denver Day

nine.

Mexico City would be a relatively
subtle location to enter the fray, we
thought. Everyone's español was
reliable. Beyond that, to avoid being
tagged as low-hanging fruit by average
bears in the land of Montezuma, the
more general sufficiency of our wisdom
regarding the hegemons of geography and
culture was a calculated gamble.

Sam and I found work at a café
diner in Coyoacán while Red spent most
of her days at Biblioteca Central
U.N.A.M. The university provided an
excellent intellectual backdrop for
networking and research. And also
recruiting, frankly. Hey, nobody in
their right mind turns down honest,
competent help. When encountered, to
hire the Buddha's a no-brainer.

It was possible that we'd end up

308

in the more northerly latitudes, e.g.
Tamaulipas or Coahuila. There was and
is plenty of apeshit going on in
northern Mexico's land-based black
market shipping lanes, such as the area
known regionally as The Golden Triangle
which angles into Tejas. I was always
instructed those export routes were,
historically, less dangerous along the
international border regions to the
west of the Lone Star State. On the
other hand, without helicopters, we had
no reason to anticipate any jobs south
of Mexico. Understandably disregarding
confused international policy,
narcotics cartels continue their
diversification in the global market to
strengthen economic footholds, so maybe
we'd end up somewhere on the coast
where grassroots and ad hoc
international policy come together
despite N.A.F.T.A., C.A.F.T.A.,
P.N.T.R., or the T.P.P.

We were just as willing to send a

hatful of bipeds down to davey jones in
the Gulf of California as we'd been to
plant a half-dozen at a dive bar in
Boulder although it was unclear how the
three of us might commandeer an ocean-
class freight vessel using just elbow
grease and a baseball bat or whatever.
But stranger things have happened.

Strong boners come easily to me
regarding illicit or pirated mining or
oil production and export. I, you, the
hegemons of hegemons and hegemony, and
the hegemons of galactic ecological
normality which is a high court of the
cosmos, all have legitimate interests
regarding resources derived from the
essence of a terrestrial mount. Any
taking of precious things from our
living platform must be auditable,
orderly, and sustainable, not endless,
blind nighthauls by the fuckload to
inland China for the purpose of dumping
it all into the Yangtzee River from the
Three Gorges Dam until everyone's

irradiated, suffocating on burnt lead,
and fried to a crisp. What we on earth
know as oceans can disappear overnight,
according to my green dreams. Mars
indeed. You think the moon's a harsh
mistress? Try doing without the tide.

Consider this local North American
example. Each car with which one
shares the road has a Vehicle
Identification Number stamped on a
little metal strip in the dash. The
tin for that V.I.N. strip and the
rest of the car doesn't grow on trees.
Materially, the automobile is a very
special thing, whether appropriated
from a llantera up the road or the
dealership on Main Street, or, whether
it has (aluminum) license plates, or
paper ones which the owner fabricates
to avoid the bitch from Illinois at the
D.M.V. who runs illegal warrant
checks. And the like. These people
are cannibals.

Denver Day

Anyway a legitimate, auditable
operation should be answerable for the
production of any such vehicle in
conformance with the overarching
marketplace parameters as well as the
physical realities of vehicles in
motion. But that's not possible if
cocaine-mustachioed South American
mariners are conspiring with chain-
smoking reds in Land's End jackets,
amid negotiations by which blow jobs
and greenbacks are the key factors for
determining who will own and regulate
the means of terrestrial resource
production. W.T.F., right? If they
were shipping out solar cells or
something else with actual merit, I'd
lighten up remarkably. Maybe that's
happening too, but I say they're still
in too deep with the mail-order brides
and nose candy.

Mexico is a beautiful country with
a rich and vast culture and I take
issue with idiots and morons down there

turning it into a deathwound. It must
stop. Then again, so should all the
dipshit nonsense which is just as bad
in the States.

Having deployed ourselves
successfully, we watched, waited,
worked, and studied in Tenochtitlan.
Any timing was perfect timing. Our
first call was in September.

eight.

We were cautious with our ad hoc
foreign service pro bono. Yes, we were
integrating successfully, yes we were
operating a merit-based joint venture
in good faith, yes we were pacifico but
we also knew, anyone wanting to be
friends with the fishy Americanos
without due cause could be a troll or
naïve or worse. Down in Mexico City we
couldn't talk out of school all night
long at the local diner while playing

cards and sketching on napkins. Not
necessarily. But we did.

All politics are local, vuelta y
vuelta. The bottom dollar, how the end
turns out, the last detail, the way of
the gun, or standing judgment relies on
frank, intellectual communication
whether in Mexico City or Denver or
Naabeehó Bináhásdzo, and if you have
something worthwhile to contribute to
the dialog it doesn't matter where
you're from or where you're going. So
went our regular nightline café diner
conversations in Coyoacán with odd
assortments of locals, shop owners,
baristas, U.N.A.M. faculty members,
etc. Business is business, and travels
bring like-minded thought. We made
some cool friends but we weren't
sleeping with them.

Provided with proper quarter, we
had no reason to consider ourselves any
less capable or ready than we'd been in

Phoenix, Baltimore, or Denver. It was
the same kind of work and the technical
risk exposure was also close. The
style of local law enforcement and
government were similar, and the soft
double-blind nature of our command
chain was intact. The work had the
same philosophical foundations and
involved the same core personnel, and
so on. And if any assignment was too
hairy, we were free to decline.

In university towns, if a market
provides the blow, the kids will blow
it. I mean to say, one should have no
problem moving a kilo or whatever in a
college town whether it's Ohio or
Caracas. The first few details were
local, and exceptionally softball jobs,
hedgework like process service and
fencing. It's not flashy, but readily
available for the cautious and
competent. Homeowners Association
footwork which we did graciously while
enjoying the scenery.

Denver Day

We survived the first relatively
dicey situation of our Mexican tenure
on what would've been Thanksgiving in
the U.S.A.

seven.

It was fitting and proper that we
nearly bought it on such a colonialist
holiday. We took a job out in
Veracruz, testing the limits of our
comfort zone and pushing beyond the
D.F. In some ways, it compared to the
Boulder affair. It was a one night
round trip.

A longer expedition to the north
would've been problematic in at least
three ways. First, the northern
reaches of Mexico are the farthest away
from the federal seat of government,
closer to U.S.A. It's a geopolitical
thing. There's also the rugged and

arid terrain to consider; Mexico's not
all temperate meadows and beaches. The
past rarely finds exception to
mountains being more effective borders
than arbitrary lines on a map. And
regarding the north, once they're so
far up into the hinterlands, the
attitudes of smugglers can change worse
for the darker, since they're closer to
the fence of the land of the free and
further from the implied trappings of
urbane business practices.

Our instructions were to make a
burn of a beach deal, exchanging hot
lead for heroin. It went down like
that too, pretty much, but for our
being shot at while leaving. We were
on foot when that happened, which was
quite different than being shot at in a
car. But we got through it.

Here's how that all went down:
Having rented a car we left the capital
city and made the departing trip in one

leg, carrying the nine-millimeter Lugers delivered to our rental address earlier that year. We even packed beachwear though we never used it.

Heaters are clean, effective, and fast, and one doesn't have to touch anyone. We'd been provided with Bowie knives too, nice ones with sheathes, whetstones, and oil. Blades are quiet, and as foreigners with a compelling interest in maintaining a low profile, we'd learned to use them whenever possible. But if the overall operation in Veracruz went correctly, it wouldn't matter how much fucking noise we made.

Maybe the civil corps hadn't gotten the memo about three gringos visiting for the purpose of mowing down a few narcotraficantes a la playa. Or maybe they did, and that's why they overshot us instead of picking us off, which they could have done easily. Anyway, someone fired shots over our head, as we returned to the car.

It was a morning deal, so we
stayed the night in Tampico, woke
early, and made our way to Pueblo Viejo
via Puente Tampico bridge, under which
we put down three dudes. That morning,
near a jetty at a waterfront rendezvous
our role was of buyers. We were shown
a sample of product, and eagerly
advised that boatloads more of it were
readily available. En español, Sam
told them our briefcase for payment was
in the car. A scant moment later she
broke leather, and dropped one of them
as Red and I took down the other two.

Pro tip: During an illicit
transaction, if you have strange
liaisons ever "going to the car"
under the pretense of retrieving
something, always become alert. That's
free advice.

The heroin, packaged in an Igloo-

brand cooler, remained in the sand
where its purveyors had set it. Our
job was done and as we started back to
the car, we heard an automatic weapon
firing. Rat-tat-tat-tat-tat-tat, like
a woodpecker, you know. At first it
sounded like the shots might have been
too far away, but lead's lead so
without further data, just sounding far
doesn't mean jack.

From that point, it wasn't far to
the car. We ran like hell. I never
spotted the origin of the shots, but I
could hear the rifle rounds swishing
through the air above us. We made it
because someone let us. Saying hello.
Friendly communications. Maybe even a
little in-kind cover.

"They could have had us with that
assault rifle." Red said. "Easy."

"Tacit support isn't bad news.
But the sentiment could change with the

weather." I said.

So the warning salute was but a
friendly audit, as far as we could
tell, and the six-hour trip home went
well enough.

Whether here or back in the States
or anywhere else, as we persisted in
this sort of work we became ever more
likely, statistically, to be zeroed.
Such inevitabilities aren't binding
among the hegemons, though. I tried to
estimate whether we might retire down
there, wind up just cooling it in Old
Mexico for thirty to fifty years. The
word "retire" means different things
to different people, however; I'm not
talking the deep philosophy of fate,
I'm just talking a decades-long siesta
in the horse latitudes.

The duplicitous philosophical
nature of life kept turning the mind.
To keep death at arm's length is to be

intimate with it, like at the courtship level, hence the aforementioned solution of dealing with it as "not-death." I considered, that if one's activities truly don't matter except for aesthetic value, which is probably true to some extent or another, then serving the aesthetic form is a key to right meaningful living. The implication was that the three of us, like Jules, had to be aware of the time in order to work the clock effectively. Death is change, that's all, and a firm grasp of that fact increases one's attention to timing. There's free agency available and things don't have to go down any particular way.

Nevertheless, time and life can be squandered, so make hay while the sun shines. The world spins like a wheel of roulette and life's an open market. There's a difference between playing with an agenda and playing with intent, as the former approach betrays a common

misunderstanding of the marketplace.
One easy way to up the auntie for the
sake of the game, and at the pleasure
of the hegemons of sex and death, was
for us to recruit local wildlife, of
which the local taxonomy was richly
diverse.

six.

   Life's all about opportunities;
To meet or seek none further is another
viable definition for actual death. As
a journo (well, a former journalist
turned antinarcotics antihero), I
still had an itch for political effect.
Hence, location was a key factor of
whether or not we stayed in Mexico. I
was mindful of where we'd been, where
we were going, what was accomplished,
and what might require further effort.
Such a searching attitude colors one's
daily business, and opportunities for
transcendental cash-in of one's own

self must also be weighed seriously and implemented without hesitation if required. Mine is just one school of thought on that subject; by my standard it's always a part of the equation, a part of the definition of "dedication" and "guaranty."

One interesting aspect of metaphysical accountability in operating policy is that such terminal factors aren't belabored in hegemonic venues. Any high court of sex and death, for example, is a terminal state in its own right. By the time any issue is pressed into an end-run of ultimate consequence, the census of the living or dead is already settled. Death is subordinate to justice and poses no obstacle for summoning witnesses or any other service. Death is a parlor game for those awaiting dockets.

Operationally, proper planning and

style of approach usually accommodate
serendipity and other tractable
alternatives to net-negative results.
This perspective fits in with the
previously described imprisonment
mindfulness practice. Notwithstanding
streetlight effect, it's unlikely that
one's own actual subjective death will
happen in any given situation.
Objective death is a separate subject
and seems to happen constantly since it
denotes nothing more than mastery or
obscuration of particular local foci.
So death may be bulletproof but in my
experience there's always a real risk
of imprisonment.

Also, the dharma preserves its
preferred agents even amid cataclysm.
Fate or the numbered fates won't serve
up prejudiced trumps without due cause
and proper compensation. In hindsight,
I see key events and unique occurrences
as contingent on the ascendance of Tex.
Even now, all I need to do is catch a

fire for an audience with her. I don't know what other various pots she still has on the stove, but I know she hooked my ass up for sure. Someone, probably some iteration of herself, offered a deal she couldn't refuse and she tendered it in my passenger seat under I-95.

When one's life is a neverending fishing expedition like mine, it's difficult to blend in with the common trout. But who cares, really? Life's not a fucking soap opera. Not a shitty one, anyway. One challenge of hedging on futures is to retain the widest range of forward-looking opportunities, to avoid the restrictive labeling of oneself that locks out certain paths or goals. Some creatures frown upon my lack of what I consider to be undue commitment, but my habitual problem with commitment is rooted in the avoidance of such pigeonholing. Believe me I'm committed, but not to

any hell's half acre of some confused
pilgrim whose condescending frowns are
a warning of their nearsighted designs
on my future.

How to configure such policy most
effectively, efficiently, and
desirably? On the way home from
Veracruz, these items rattled around in
my head like seeds in a dried gourd.
To the extent that one can know the
answers, I pondered our best options
pursuant to them and regarding what
might be done to freshen up the outlook
if nothing seemed clearly enticing. I
had a feeling one of our new buddies
from the U.N.A.M. could help with our
political fine tuning. There'd be risk
in that, but worth it.

I was sold on the idea by the time
we returned to Coyoacán. One likely
catch involved with bringing on new
staff would be deviation from narcotics
interdiction, since we were less likely

to find people specialized exactly as
we were.

five.

Our plurality was part of our in-
plain-view M.O. and an exception to
the general rule that people in this
line of work operate alone.

We were obvious white hats,
functionally, which is still
effectively a black hat in the blind
eyes of most people. Let's just say
gray suit. And flip-flops. In any
case, we'd already made individual
contacts within the local talent pool
and were parsing a known quantity for
our farm-in.

Family's forever and business is
for life, so adding staff is an
elective process because it's never
absolutely necessary to add anyone at

all. One must choose carefully.
There's risk to growth, in fact it's
pure risk but if it suits, one adds
while minimizing borrowed trouble with
care. We wouldn't add people without
our own feather and we sure as hell
weren't adding people we didn't enjoy.

Risk of conceding the moral high
ground was of more concern to me than
potential deviation from our narcotics
specialty. Being on foreign soil
complicated the ethical measure of the
matter, but not so far as to prevent
fundamental justifications. I, we,
were still making a universal
implementation of our belief system.
Regardless of the current geography,
ethics remained a key factor of our
operating budget and we needed to
retain a pristine philosophical
mooring, hence the necessity of knowing
and liking one's committed partners.

Conversely, for the ethical

incorporation of natural rights,
legalistic exclusivity of locality and
geography can be vacated. Foreigners
are often not thought of as neighbors
but they are people. Because we're all
people, ethical omission can be a grave
offense. Failure to stop and render
aid has been viewed as a crime for long
ages, even by the Romulans albeit
cynically.

We'd made some friends from the
art department, and some from the
philosophy faculty, and some journalism
people also. I, Red, and Sam talked
over the merits of our various new
friends and eliminated all preferred
candidates except the philosophy guy.
The Mexican patriotism of our
journalism faculty liaison and his
colleagues limited their usefulness or
accessibility to us, because their
position carried too much proclivity
for exchanging an ethical point for
sheer nationalism. But we could still

be friends. Again, regardless of
constituent nation states, it was our
specialization or focus which was
flexible, not our ethical lines.

The art faculty was useful for its
ontological proximity to black market
logistics and aesthetic truth. For the
same reasons, however, its interests
were too easily conflated with those of
narcotics operators and adversarial
black market intelligence operatives.

Julian Santana was our philosophy
guy, an associate professor at
U.N.A.M., whose family from Veracruz
was involved in the offshore oil and
gas business segment. We hung out with
Julian at a local café in Coyoacán
where Sam was working. He liked us
because we could communicate with him
on a philosophical level, and because
he could use us to brush-up on his
Shakespeare. His English was at least
as good as Sam's, Red's, and my

Denver Day

Spanish. Sam and he also talked to
each other en français, and so on. His
Russian was horrible. Red and he
tested their Mandarin on each other in
conversations indistinguishable from
questionable art. Aesthetics in
semantics is critical for avoidance of
epistemological hells. It's not a
silver bullet but it's a part of the
solution.

    We didn't really have a plan for
him and didn't require him for any of
our local work, but he was available
and practical. Shall I define fate as
knowing one's self and one's work well
enough to enable the proper selection
of mates, where doing so in the context
of persistent right effort avails true
paths? I perceive paths of truth are
themselves living, therefore, they're
responsive and intelligent. Rivers are
alive and so is the ground and they
offer real wisdom.

four.

Near the solstice, the rising sun
illuminated a new partnership after six
hours of playing gin with Julian and a
khaki-skinned woman with obsidian eyes
named Marla, who was his teaching
assistant. Two weeks later, he pitched
a deal at us.

Julian's work was focused on
linguistics, the nuances of which may
have been beyond our necessary suite of
blunt objects, but we welcomed any
addition of witcraft and he was a true
paisano. Our disposition isn't unique
and one knows one's own. I expected
he'd enlighten us per some novel aspect
of the Mexican political will; he
didn't disappoint.

Basically, his people out in el
Golfo de México were, ahh, ummm,
"decommissioning" certain offshore

Denver Day

rigs on short notice   (that's his
punctuation;   whenever he said the
word, he always gesticulated quotation
marks with his fingers).   A key concern
pursuant to Mexico's governing interest
was regarding how best to perform such
rapid decomm operations with ecological
mindfulness.   The President of the
Republic, Mexican Navy, Pemex, and the
gulf's at-large marine life et al,
didn't want any unnecessary burning
hell disaster coming down in the
G.O.M.

In case you didn't know,
industrial decommissioning is a
fundamental aspect of the engineering
lifecycle, and there are right and
wrong ways to do it.   An example of the
wrongest way is to blowout the well and
scuttle the platform, as in the eco-
nightmare hackjob of Deepwater Horizon
offshore Macondo 2010.

Generally fucking local seas and

334

global oceans is a high crime and
heinous act of war, as a matter of
fact. It's one of the ways
interplanetary corporate warfare is
prosecuted. Where no individual agent
is consequential enough to qualify as a
target, as is the case frequently, the
ecosystems themselves take the hit.
Which incidentally clears the platform
of local agency. Believe that.
Anyway, there are orderly ways to pull
and cap those wells without spilling a
drop.

"I can get behind this deal for
sure." said Red.

"Did they teach you about this
kind of thing at the police academy?"
Sam asked her.

"Not as such. But some aspects of
the training might come in handy."

That was that. We'd graduated to

Denver Day

new moral high ground on the high seas,
being tasked with actionable maritime
intelligence alongside the philosophy
professor's Veracruz-based familia.
There was no foreseeable reason to stop
at the Gulf of Mexico since most wells
are wildcat wells, it's a big world,
and nobody shucks our corn but us. The
appropriate perspective regarding
wildcatters is, they're big assholes
who want to put a rod right into your
mom. I am very broadly defining
wildcatter to mean every well including
Spindletop. Somebody get me a map.
Your earth is alive and has the same
civil rights as you.

    We sat up that night amid the
lovely ancient not-winter of the
Aztecs, eyeballing our fresh crossroads
with glad smiles.

three.

Hipster Bricks

The Santana contract was maritime
business as usual for organizations
with such interests. Among the guilds
of resource administration, cohesion is
necessary for establishing and
maintaining global hegemony in
technology, security, economy,
egalitarianism, and conservation.
These considerations are the named
price for hegemons of local order,
terrestrial and otherwise.

We know all politics are local.
Mines, hydrocarbons, libraries,
museums, and other civil infrastructure
must be undefiled. Be overly cautious
of out-of-town investors. Only insofar
as they want your ass do they want your
money. Carpetbaggers are hip to the
fact that script currency lacks actual
value, beyond their inclination for it
which is increased market leverage for
interlopers such as themselves. If
they're bad-faith operators, they don't
belong and you don't want them in your

sphere of influence, whether it's a geopolitical state or a state of being and probably both. They want to drink your blood.

Anyway, our new gig with Julian sounded fancy and was a new kind of adventure for us, but from what I gathered, it was typical maritime support and there would be none of our standard murder-in-the-dark action. Then again, the work we'd grown accustomed to was gory only in the literal sense.

Our not being actual mariners wasn't an issue. They needed technicians. Data crunchers and general staff. Competent, discreet, international partisans to cover sensitive administrative or logistical details of offshore operations. We were put to those efforts immediately and learned much about offshore Mexico's Golden Lane fields, such as

the ownership details of the infrastructure. It's worth noting, paper
money does contribute affirmatively to
the important cause of keeping various
morons out of the copper mines despite
my endless bellyaching about
currencies. It's a challenge for me
not to view a stack of dollars as a
stack of warrants (or as someone
else's unresolved and unorganized
casework).

Citing business reasons, Julian's
father intimated to me that he didn't
like "those cacahuates down in Rio."
The Brazilian real has built enormous
energy infrastructure offshore Brazil,
and created an international investment
and production boom. At this very
time, there's a totally unnecessary
international clusterfuck of corporate
jackals pillaging those waters and
making a mess. Offshore Africa's an
even bigger disaster. The problem is
global.

Of course the same can be said for Mexico's Golden Lane, and in the U.S. regions of the Gulf of Mexico, and among the various partisan claims to the North Sea, and throughout the waters of the Asian Pacific, and on and on. Santana and associates' efforts would have been like a search for a needle in a needle stack, except it was a fairly well-mapped stack so the needles they wanted were easily located.

For any paramilitary operation, to get the job done entirely by way of intelligence is the most ideal, least risky, cleanest, and easiest approach. A peaceable strategic approach is ever the secondary option. Shutting down offshore production takes standard mothballing and decommissioning protocol, properly planned and peopled. The green army, for lack of a better institutional catch-all term, might

offer advice and historical perspective
for such efforts. If there isn't a
peaceful change in command on location,
the next best option can be quantified
in terms of minimum tactical personnel
eliminations. If not zero, then one
would be the preferred tally for such
efforts. And so on.

   Not only is the wildcat offshore
drilling at a riotous pitch today but
the seas are also crowded with leaky
F.P.S.O. projects which are over-ripe
for fair and proper decommissioning.
Anyway, because there is so much work
to be done, there's a certain ubiquity
to it. Final determinations on an
offshore platform about the last cop
out during a peaceable civil change of
national operating standard is
practically indistinguishable from the
casual social or dramatic blocking
that's par for cocktail parties.
Otherwise, it's someone taking a long
walk off a short pier. Not very fancy,

Denver Day

huh?

   Alas, we were never asked to join
a boarding party or even leave dry
land. It was an office job, literally.
The technical nature of the job was an
interesting, redeemable aspect of the
content, which kept us from getting
bored and walking off in search of more
stimulating ways to liaison with the
hegemons of ecology.

   That story summarizes the comings
and goings of our organization around
that New Year. Julian still scribbled
relentlessly into notebooks about
metaphysics and linguistics, and we all
continued our late night cards and tea
at our favorite local café diner,
enjoying our compatriots, confederates,
comrades, and colleagues. Again, the
not-winter of Coyoacán is a dream.

two.

Maybe it's not ironic that we never left our cubes working for the Santanas. But we could write on our resumes "support services for a privately held, Distrito Federal-based, naval operation." It is an interesting notch in the belt and there must be plenty of foreign service personnel who only dream of landing such a sweet gig. Our own accidental D.I.Y. moxy, ever evolving from its original deviation, is what had put us where we were. In fact, I was concerned that if the ride upward with a bullet continued, one of us might end up in public office.

Answerable to no one and nothing except grand ideologies, we were accidental public servants, where earlier in the journey the only things to worry about had been death and jail. Since we'd inadvertently become part of the commonweal, life had grown more complicated while death and jail had

somehow become part of a slippery slope
upwards, ironically. We meant well,
yet we had become bureaucrats and
bureaucracies are dangerous. There's
been a bureaucracy at the root of every
horrible thing that's ever happened;
The more people inside an organization,
the greater is its perceived need to
control outside individuals or groups.

There is an undeniable fishy
feeling when one's path has gone
through hell, high water, bullet
wounds, transcendental enlightenment,
and general international romping only
to wind up in some office pushing
pencils. Sort of comfortable yet odd
generally. That's what things had come
to. A far cry from working alone, but
form follows function and it didn't
matter anyway because a sea change was
faithfully overdue.

It's never any problem to locate
some hazardous, poorly lit snake pit to

dive into, no matter how far up the
soft-ass air-conditioned loop-de-loop
one has shimmied. Actually seeking out
trouble to jump in isn't necessary
because nature will ambush when given
leave to do so (trying to fend off
nature only postpones the inevitable.)
There is an art to rolling with such
organic attacks for the purpose of
surviving them.

My argument to the partners was,
we couldn't stay in Mexico City
forever, cushy job or not. I must
sound like a broken record, I know.
They said so, but they also knew I was
right. I stayed on with Julian through
the rest of the dry season, then pulled
out for some "me" time. Sam and Red
continued on with the cubicle farm, and
our living and playing together
continued. I worked a few jobs through
Red, as I'd been doing since the day we
met in Colorado. I was working alone
again, quiet work.

Denver Day

I did a lot of writing, no
surprise there. My activities had long
since become too sensitive or
potentially incriminating for verbatim
record keeping but there's always a
green light for decent fiction. And,
things did soon enough change again,
after a fashion which you may perceive
as drastic, although such apprehension
is to misunderstand the nature of
change, as I always say.

It turned out that in June, one
particular job would be my last one of
the sort. I still work out, if you
will, but my relationship with the
world and its hegemons is changed.
Like Jules', my work has taken on a
more administrative nature. Basically
I was shot and killed but not buried.
I know that sounds like bullshit. It
surprised me too, but hear me out.
This final tale of the day explains
much about Jules' civil status,

foregoing and otherwise, and belies odd esoterics about the little organization some refer to as "the world." The story may also render the faces of the hegemons more clearly.

The last detail was thus: I was supposed to meet some dude in a fairly sketchy section of the city and conduct incidental reconnaissance. A fishing expedition combined with a burn. It was a scenario where the best calculations required a lone casualty, having been whittled down in good faith, to just one person on the business end. I went to the meeting point and waited outside some laundry joint. The person arrived on time and things were going as planned.

We went to the back office. There were a few people in the building who were supposed to be there, for the sole purpose of providing me with general cover, which meant they were expecting

Denver Day

a body and prepared to deal with it.
Instead, there would be at least two
gippers, however I stopped my fretting
about carcass logistics after someone
put me down like an old mule, with a
high velocity slug into the back of my
head. It happens. Such is the nature
of things, do not be alarmed.

Anyway, I'm in the laundromat with
this coke dealer. We went to the back
office which was empty except for
several kilo bricks of product sitting
on a card table. I made a little small
talk before shooting him several times
in the chest. I stood over him and put
two more rounds into the head, then
felt a cold barrel at the base of my
own skull. There was thunder and I was
offline.

one.

Biological parameters can be

348

compromised at any moment, so it's
important to develop the mind while
physical opportunities and tools are
better accessible. We make hay while
the sun shines.

Being shot, point blank in the
base of the skull, scratched an itch
that had been slightly beyond reach to
me for forty-one years. It was also
very jarring. My normal graphical user
interface was interrupted immediately,
as I mentioned, yet a clear awareness
remains, and that's just the beginning.

Immediately I knew what had
happened. For a short while, I still
received and processed bio-net signal
through what was left of the brain
core, whose processing function dropped
fast to zero, after the direct physical
trauma to it and the halt of vascular
function. There was no pain, but the
ears rang at all frequencies and
colors, as one expects at such a close

proximity to the discharge of a
firearm. The ringing faded with the
rapid progression of neural function
loss, and of course much faster than it
would've otherwise. So, each
cognizable reduction in noise signal
overload felt like main switches going
off, terminating nerve channels. Soon
the body was only a discarded meat
jacket and the decomposition began.

The contents of the mind, however,
remain faithfully intact afterward,
outside of the physical incorporation.
Live well because those contents will
carry on. In fact, they're more easily
accessible without the communications
and memory limitations of individually
fixed integrated modules. Time is now
of a wholly different essence and
perspective is changed drastically.

One of several keys for surviving
death is to properly sever attachment
or reliance on an erstwhile bio-

mechanoid, the clinging to which is like powering a fried motherboard or re-shelling an egg; Yes, either can be done theoretically, but it's a last resort.

Enlightenment is described by Zen scholars as seeing one's own face before one's parents were born. The point is, it's still you. But what of it? Although death isn't necessary for enlightenment, it's a crucial part of education. Do you find it comforting to know consciousness remains? If one's existence is a nightmare, maybe it isn't comforting.

I keep saying change is the only constant and that's certainly true of life. It's true of death too, but one reason life and living is in constant flux is, the dead have a capacity for yet slower, relatively still momentum around which quicker currents flow. Having learned to change in the quick,

one may also swim effectively beyond
it. Otherwise, the stop-motion of
failed mechanicals begets a creep of
festering transcendental rot. Such are
the benchmarks of biology and forward
progress. Differences in levels of
philosophical preparedness among
generations, civilizations, or entire
epochs shed light upon law and
jurisprudence and is exactly why karmic
or constitutional law is binding beyond
the living and profane.

   Remarkably, along with the
auditory overload, I experienced a
brief physical vision of infinitely
brilliant colors with the last blast.
It was a helluva rainbow, such is
violent head trauma. As the signal
faded, I discovered my consciousness
was already reorganized enough for me
to recount the sequence of events.
Being so rapidly re-coalescing after
those colorful moments, soon I was able
to settle into what I've found to be my

new standard state of being, awareness, and perception. So far.

Since there's no individual objective, physical vision is one of many things that are completely different on the other side. This aspect, like the philosophical preparedness aforementioned, is also forensically teachable and universally relevant because the biases incidental to a fixed vantage can be overcome with practice and preparation. Vision unincorporated isn't an objective vantage at all, but instead like a web or hierarchy of perspectives. Without the trappings of the body, one may shine in and out of times and locations as needed. Elective presence. The freedom is nice.

zero.

I knew my soul would live and the

affirmation was a welcome, permanent
disposition, well worth the wait.
Don't rush out, regardless of variable
terrestrial longevity, as painful and
challenging as it can be. Take the
time for living to interact, meet, and
connect with others. Moment for moment
enjoy, because I tell you that's the
sort of useful existence which is
physically accessible to shiners like
me and Jules. Among the cosmology, or
in any other transcendental sense,
peaceable, empathetic, real people
leading genuine lives are the coin of
the realm.

　　　The elementals, cosmic oceans,
celestial neighborhoods, and aesthetic
matrices are exquisite but all return
to sand in time. Edifice provides
grounds for polyphonic assembly, but
brighter than any artful shadows are
the entities casting them. That's a
fact. We're it, among others, so live
your life accordingly.

Since I'd left the body that served me so well over the decades, I wanted to sing it home, so I stuck around to see what they did with it. The guy who shot me left through the entrance we'd both used, then through a different door entered some other dude who seemed to be expecting bodies. He put me and the man I'd just killed in the same bag, carried it outside, placed it in the trunk of an old beat-up Mazda, drove to a nearby junkyard, and flung the bag into the back of a junked pickup truck that contained several other dubious black parcels.

Would I have preferred a more proper treatment like what Tex got at that fire station in Baltimore? The matter isn't without value or consequence. What happens to meat jackets can be relevant, but not a dealbreaker compared with overarching failure to recognize the soul.

Denver Day

    The collective consciousness is
infinitely full of enlightened souls
time out of mind, although there is no
overcrowding where such light prevails.
Of course there are realms crowded with
unenlightened beings too, such is
darkness. A remarkable aspect of
anthropogeny is that everyone is
philosophically present, excepting a
few notable demographics like hungry
ghosts, secularly excommunicated
untouchables, and the living lost.
These latter terms all translate the
same way, which belies a dubious
teleology; they are the penitent. I
challenge you to find any written
record of their cardinal offenses.

    Besides bad faith agency, one of
the few actual dangers in the universe
is accidental, by way of simply
forgetting that one's soul is safe and
will carry on happily, forever. In
misunderstanding death as easily

survivable, or forgetting it, people are vulnerable to the hustle against which simple faith in oneself does ensure.

Excepting preference and personal affairs, whether I attended to Red's and Sam's souls didn't matter to them whatsoever. But in light of my new role in the organization, as I had when faced with Jules' sudden change in civil status, Sam and Red had some recognitions of their own to reflect on. There were also various policy considerations for me to make, to include decisions about my level of involvement in the affairs of the living business partners. Of course, I would commit as needed, one reason being that I had all the time in the world.

My failing to watch my own back enabled a screwup that wasn't supposed to happen. The dude at the laundromat

Denver Day

had been looking for a body but he got
an extra, which was no problem as far
as he cared. So, Mr. Clean reported no
major problems at the scene, and news
of my liberated status was delayed in
getting to Red. By the time it became
obvious I was missing, I'd returned to
them in essence. I and Jules sleep
with the fishes now.